PRIDE AFTER HER FALL

BY

LUCY ELLIS

First published in Great Britain 2013
by Mills & Boon, an imprint of Harlequin (UK) Limited.
Large Print edition 2013
Harlequin (UK) Limited, Eton House,
18-24 Paradise Road, Richmond, Surrey TW9 1SR

© Lucy Ellis 2013

ISBN: 978 0 263 23197 7

Harlequin (UK) policy is to use papers that are natural,
renewable and recyclable products and made from
wood grown in sustainable forests. The logging and
manufacturing process conform to the legal environmental
regulations of the country of origin.

Printed and bound in Great Britain
by CPI Antony Rowe, Chippenham, Wiltshire

For Bridie

CHAPTER ONE

NASH as a rule didn't court publicity, so meeting with a publicist went against the grain. But this was for a charity event and he couldn't very well say no.

'I'll meet her at the American Bar in the Hotel de Paris.'

He checked his watch as he approached his low slung Bugatti Veyron.

'I'll be with Demarche until one. I can give her a couple of minutes in the bar. I'll try to make it, but she may have to cool her heels.'

It was one of the few perks of fame. People would wait. He hooked the door of the Veyron and idled for a moment, looking out over the calm Mediterranean water.

Cullinan was talking about seating.

'No, mate, don't book a table. This is a five-minute job. Nobody will be sitting down.'

Blue's management team was headed up by John Cullinan, a savvy Irishman Nash had used in his early racing career when he was thrust onto the world stage. John had protected him from the worst of the media for over a decade and he trusted him to deal fairly with the public and handle the professionals.

He'd need him in the coming weeks. There was already intense speculation about his future. He hadn't said a word during the running of the Grand Prix here in Monaco in May, but somehow just his presence trackside with current Eagle heavyweight Antonio Abruzzi had sent the media into a frenzy. Not that it took much. Meat in the water and the piranhas swarmed. That was why this meeting with the construction firm Eagle was taking place in the privacy of a hotel room and security barracudas on both sides had had elaborate lock-down procedures in place.

He ended the call and jumped into the Veyron, keen to get out of town.

The flip of a wrist and he had the engine purring. His deep-set blue-grey eyes, which one female sports commentator had called *'lethal blue'* as if they not only needed colour coding but branding, assessed the traffic and he pulled away from outside the corporate offices of the business that had been his heart and soul for five years.

He had just tied up a deal with Swiss-based car manufacturer Avedon to produce Blue 22, and whilst every vehicle design was a rush this was the car he'd first conceptualised back in his racing days, when nobody would have taken him seriously if he'd spilled his guts on his future plans.

Fortunately he'd never been overly chatty. Being raised by a mean drunk who'd seen a kid's prattle as an excuse to deal out backhanders had bred in him the habit of silence. To the public he was notoriously impenetrable. 'Self-contained,' one journalist reported. 'A cold sonafabitch,' countered a disenchanted former lover.

But, however else he was perceived, the world took him seriously nowadays even when they weren't intrusively curious. At thirty-four, he'd survived as a professional in one of the most dangerous sports in the world for almost a decade before retiring in a blaze of glory—and unlike so many sports pros he'd parlayed his expertise and a passionate love of design into a second career.

An extremely successful second career.

One that overshadowed whatever fame he'd had as a driver—which had been his intention. He could command any price for his work and right now he was in demand—at the top of an elite field of specialists.

Yet he was restless, there was no denying that, and several times in the last year he'd caught himself asking the fateful question: What next?

But he knew the answer to that question. It was why the Eagle head honchos had flown in last night.

Yeah, he wanted back in the game, but this time on his own terms. His twenties had gone past in a rush of track groupies and speed as he'd raced against the world's best and outraced his own demons. He'd known when it was time to stop. He also knew this time it would be different. He wasn't a boy any more. His feelings about racing had undergone a change. He had nothing to prove.

The road cleared. He changed gear and took off up the hill.

He had a date this morning up on the Point, with a genuine glamour-girl car who had it all over this newer model he was driving, and even the stumbling block of dealing with meetings all afternoon couldn't dull the edge of what promised to be a very nice find. She was reported to be a sweet little number, with curves aplenty, an all-original and he was finally going to see what the fuss was about.

She'd only recently come on the market, and Nash knew he'd have to move quickly, but he didn't buy without handling the merchandise.

He'd flown in to Monaco that morning after twenty-four hours in the air to hear the news that the owner had loaned her out but she'd be available to look at this afternoon. With the morning to kill he'd decided to take the opportunity to run up the hill and possibly rescue the poor thing from whatever indignities had been visited upon her overnight.

The place overlooked the bay—nice and exclusive. But what address *wasn't* exclusive in this town? The house had a little fame for being a silent-film actress's hideaway in the twenties and he was a little curious to see it. He'd driven past many times, but this was the first occasion he'd had to turn in, idling at the gates—which, to his surprise, were wide open. Security was usually pretty tight in this neck of the woods.

As he eased the sports car down the linden lined gravel drive he slowed to a creep, taking in the state of disrepair. Masses of flowering bougainvillaea couldn't hide the fact that the old place needed a face-job.

And then he saw her.

Nash barely had his car at a standstill before he was out, slamming the door, advancing on the object of his desire.

Sticking out of a flowerbed.

A 1931 Bugatti T51, currently upended in a parterre of small flowered bushes. As if to add to the indignity one of its doors was hanging open.

Every muscle in his body stiffened. He wasn't angry. He was beyond anger.

He was *appalled*.

But he was a man who had made self-control a byword. He reined in the fury—knew it needed to be directed where it could do some good.

Coming towards him was a rotund man in garden greens, shaking his arms towards the sky as if inviting divine intercession.

'Monsieur! Un accident avec la voiture!'

Yeah, that was one way of putting it.

And that was when the shouting started.

CHAPTER TWO

LORELEI St James came awake with a languorous stretch, sliding her bare arms over silken sheets, revelling sensuously in the luxurious comfort. She made a *'mmph'* sound, rolled over and buried her face in the pillow, prepared to sleep away the day, if that were possible—only to hear a deep male voice raised in anger somewhere outside her bedroom terrace.

Ignore it, she decided, snuggling in.

The voice lifted.

She snuggled a bit more.

More shouts.

She wrinkled her nose.

A crash.

What now?

Sighing, Lorelei pushed her satin sleep mask haphazardly up her forehead and winced as she copped an eyeful of bright Mediterranean sunshine. The room did a rinse-cycle spin around her—no doubt the product of too much champagne, inadequate sleep and enough financial trouble to sink this house around her ears.

She shoved thoughts about the latter to the back of her mind even as her heart began to beat the band, and she felt about for a glass of water to ease the Sahara Desert that was her throat this morning. She was greeted by a clatter as she clumsily knocked her watch, her cell phone and a tangle of assorted jewellery to the stone floor.

Easing herself into a sitting position, pushing the fall of chin-length blond curls out of her eyes, Lorelei wrinkled her nose and held on to the mattress as the room did another gentle spin.

I will never drink again, she vowed. *Although if I do,* she revised, *only champagne cocktails... and at a pinch G&T's.*

As if sensing she was at her most vulnerable, the phone on the floor gave a judder and began to vibrate. Her heart did that annoying leap and race thing again. She made a pained face. When the phone rang nowadays there was usually somebody angry on the other end...

To dissuade her from getting out of bed it stopped, but the muted sound of male voices coming up from below her terrace lifted to a crescendo. This was what had woken her. Men shouting. Some sort of altercation going on.

Surely she didn't have to deal with this, too? Not today…

But without the catering staff from last night there was only Giorgio and his wife, Terese, and it was unfair to expect them to deal with interlopers. They'd had a lot of them in the past few weeks—all of them creditors, hunting her down now that her father Raymond was banged up in a low-security prison.

As if she had a cent to her name after two years of legal fees.

It wasn't that she was exactly ignoring her problems—she preferred to think of it as delegating responsibility. She'd deal with the phone calls later, and the emails and the lawyers who wanted her signature on a mountain of documents. Not today. Maybe tomorrow. It was just such a nice day. The sun was shining. She shouldn't ruin it. One more day in paradise and then she'd pay the piper.

Just one more day…

And then she remembered. Not only did she have a client booked in at noon, she had an appointment this afternoon at the Hotel de Paris. It was about her grandmother's charity: the Aviary Foundation. Every year they hosted an event to raise money for cancer research.

This year the feature was a one-day vintage car rally, and a famous racing driver would be giving kids struggling with cancer the pleasure of a spin around the track in a high-powered vehicle. Their usual publicist was ill, and the foundation's president had personally asked her to do the meet-and-greet with their guest celebrity.

She squeezed her temples. She hadn't even done any research. What if he expected her to know his stats? She could barely balance her own chequebook…

Last year they had lined up a Hollywood actor who famously had a home here in Monaco. Now, *that* one would have been easy—watch a few films, gush… Everyone knew actors had egos like mountains. Frowning, she contemplated racing-car drivers. Weren't they kind of like cowboys? She pictured swagger and ego in equal dimensions. *Blah.*

Reaching for the *eau de nil* silk evening gown crumpled at the foot of her bed, Lorelei tugged it over her head. Really, she was happy to do the meet-and-greet—she'd do anything the Aviary Foundation asked of her—just not today…

She gave a shriek as something small and furry tunnelled its way onto her lap, claws digging into her flesh.

'Fifi,' she admonished, pulling the silk to her waist, 'behave, *ma chere.*'

Lifting her beloved baby, she buried her face in a ball of white fluff.

'Now, be good and stay here. *Maman* has things to attend to.'

Fifi sat up expectantly in the pool of white silk sheets, curious eyes on her mistress as she opened the French doors and went to step outside. Lorelei doubled back as she remembered she wasn't wearing any underwear. She wasn't prudish about her body, but she knew Giorgio was conservative and she didn't want to embarrass him unnecessarily.

Belting her robe at the waist, Lorelei wandered out onto the terrace. It was going to be another one of those perfect early September days, and she inhaled the briny breeze filled with lavender and rosemary scents from the garden. She most definitely didn't want to go and sort this out. As she weaved her way down the stone steps, pulling her sunglasses into place, she told herself that whoever it was couldn't do anything worse than yell at her.

But it wasn't easy being shouted at, and she wondered if she was ever going to become inured to other people's anger. In her defence, she'd been facing more than her fair share lately—and it wasn't getting any easier. Maybe she was suffering from overload, because this morning it felt harder than ever. But Giorgio didn't deserve this either, and the buck had to stop somewhere.

It would just be nice if for once it didn't stop with *her*.

Lorelei saw the Bugatti first and her heart sank. How on earth had it ended up in the garden? On second thoughts, she had a pretty good idea...

And then she saw the man who had disturbed her slumber.

He was... She was...

Lorelei was vaguely aware that her mouth had formed a little 'oh' of wonder. In the next instant she remembered that she hadn't run a brush through her hair, she wasn't wearing any make-up and her panties were upstairs.

Too late now. He'd spotted her.

She couldn't do anything about her wrinkled

evening gown, but she smoothed her sleep-mussed hair, glad of the shades—which this morning were hiding a thousand sins. She tried to remember that even if she wasn't looking her best she wasn't without her own certain charm.

Besides, men were so easy.

He headed over, all six foot forever of him, with shoulders that would have served a line-backer, a deep chest, a lean waist, tight hips and long, powerful legs—and one of those classically handsome faces that made her think of old-time movie stars.

Lorelei knew better than to be a sitting target. She took the initiative and approached the Bugatti, giving her scowling uninvited guest her back view, which she knew—thanks to riding and an hour a day on her Stairmaster—wasn't bad, and came up with her best line.

'Goodness me,' she drawled, 'there's a car in my rose bushes.'

On the other hand, maybe humour hadn't been the best direction to take this in. As she listened to the crunch of gravel—big, heavy male foot-steps coming up behind her—Lorelei experi-enced that sinking feeling: the one that told her she'd read the situation all wrong.

Giorgio's expression told her to duck and cover, but after a brief, desperate glance at the older man she decided to stay where she was. It wasn't her style to cut and run, and she'd come this far—she just needed to brazen it out. And the guy had stopped shouting, which was encouraging.

'Are you responsible for this?'

Lorelei took in three things. He was Australian, he had a voice that made Russell Crowe sound like a choirboy, and—as she turned around and looked up into a set masculine face—he clearly wasn't in any mood to be amused or charmed. She couldn't blame him. The car did look pretty bad.

'*Are* you?' he repeated, snapping off his aviators and revealing a pair of spectacular eyes—navy blue rimmed with grey, surrounded by dense, thick, dark lashes.

Those eyes. They were sort of...*amazing.* Lorelei couldn't help gazing helplessly back.

Except they pinned her like a blade to a dissection board. She could almost *feel* him deciding which part of her to excise first. She came back to earth with a thump and tried to ignore the pinch in her chest. It was a look she was becoming depressingly familiar with of late, and it didn't mean anything, she told herself. She would have thought she'd be used to it by now.

He shoved the aviators into the back pocket of his jeans and settled his arms by his sides—stance widened, pure masculine intimidation.

'Anything to say for yourself?'

He was pumping out lots of frustrated testosterone, which was making her a little nervous, but she couldn't really blame him. He wanted another man to punch on the nose and he'd got her.

He clearly didn't know what to do about that.

She lifted a trembling hand and smoothed down her hair.

'Are you *high,* lady?'

Lorelei was so busy staying her ground that his questions hadn't quite penetrated, but now that he was turning away the last one landed on her with a thump.

'Pardon?'

But the guy was already focussing his entire attention back on the car, his hands on those lean, muscled hips of his as he eyed the Bugatti nose-deep in the rose bushes.

Giorgio was muttering in Italian, and the guy said something to him in his own language. Before her eyes the men appeared to be bonding over their shared outrage about the car. Freed from that penetrating stare, Lorelei frowned.

Well, really.

This wasn't how the man-meets-Lorelei scenario was supposed to play out. Her Italian was minimal, at best, and she didn't like the feeling of being forcibly held at bay by her inability to understand what was being said.

She was also a little piqued at being ignored.

And she most definitely didn't like being intimidated.

She cocked a hip, one slender hand resting just below her waist.

'So, do you think you can extract it before it does any more damage to my flowers?'

Giorgio muttered something like, *'Madonna!'*

Good—now she'd get a little action.

The man's broad shoulders grew taut, and as he turned around she felt her bravado flicker uneasily. His movements were alarmingly deliberate— as if this was *his* estate, Giorgio *his* employee and she was trespassing on *his* land. A stone-cold stare slammed into her. He suddenly seemed awfully big, and Lorelei knew in that instant he wasn't amused, he wasn't charmed and he wasn't going to be easy.

'As far as I'm concerned, lady,' he said, his expression giving no ground, 'you're screwed.'

Her reaction was fierce and immediate. She *hated* this feeling. She'd been dealing with it for too long. It felt as if all she'd done lately was shoulder the blame. So this time it was *her* fault, but for some reason his anger felt disproportionate and just plain unfair. It was too much, coming on top of everything else.

Who cared about a silly car when her life was coming apart at the seams?

So she did what she always did when a man challenged her, called her to account or tried to make himself king of her mountain. She brought out the big guns. The ones she'd learned from her beloved, irresponsible father.

Wit and sex appeal.

Lorelei dipped her glasses and gave him full wattage.

'I can hardly wait,' she purred.

CHAPTER THREE

FROM her rumpled appearance she had clearly just rolled out of bed, and for one out-of-bounds moment Nash had a strong urge to roll her back into it.

Hardly surprising. She was a striking-looking woman who exuded a sultry, knowing sensuality that could have been a combination of her looks and the way she moved her body and displayed it, but he sensed came from the essence of who she was.

In another era she would have embodied the romantic idea of a courtesan. A woman who required a great deal of money to keep the shine on her silky curls, the glow in her honeyed skin and her eyes from straying to the next main chance.

Yeah—another time and another place this could go down a lot differently.

A man like him…a woman like her…

But not today.

Not now.

And it didn't have a lot to do with the car.

With a media circus about to start up around him again, this smouldering blonde had a little bit too much attitude to burn. He might as well slap a big no-go sticker on that shapely ass of hers. She fairly neon-glowed with sex of a crazy, messy kind, and tempted as he was he couldn't afford to be indiscriminate—not this close to race-start. He'd do well to remember that.

Although his first impression of this woman had been of something quite different. When she'd first emerged for a timeless instant he'd seen only a tall, delicately built girl as graceful and hesitant as a mountain deer. She'd given him pause. For a moment there he hadn't wanted to shift a muscle in case he scared her off.

Then she'd looked right at him and headed for the Bugatti.

And right now her hands were on her hips and the glamour-girl in her was in full flow. Which was when he noticed something rather more down to earth. She wasn't wearing much. Or rather what she *was* wearing was advertising the lack of anything else.

Trying to be a gentleman, he dragged his attention upwards. But he needn't have bothered. She was clearly unfazed, and his cynicism about who she was and the price she put on herself lodged into place—because, despite his initial impression of something better, blondie was pure South of France glamour. If he upended her she probably had "Made on the Riviera" stamped on the soles of her pretty bare feet.

For a moment she'd looked a little thrown. He didn't know if she was embarrassed to be caught out or simply defensive because she didn't like being in the wrong. Frankly, he didn't care.

He cared about the car.

He whipped out his cell, punched in a number.

'As far as I'm concerned, lady, you've committed a felony. That car is a work of art and a treasure, and *you've* trashed it.'

She dragged off the huge sunglasses and a pair of pale-lashed doe eyes regarded him with a fair degree of astonishment. As if he were massively overreacting.

Nash knew he was staring back, but after the clothes and the attitude he just hadn't expected amber-brown, slightly tip-tilted, lovely... The eyes of a gentle fawn.

'I haven't trashed anything,' she countered in that low, sexy voice of hers.

Nash folded his arms, still shaking off the effect of those eyes. Somehow she was going to try and take the moral high ground. This should be good.

'It might be a little scratched—that's all,' she conceded. 'I suppose there *are* only a couple of thousand in the world—'

'Eight,' he said grimly. 'There are eight left in the world.'

For a moment he fancied he saw her take a deep swallow, but she continued on blithely, like a pretty blonde lemming running over a cliff.

'Seven more than this one—not such a catastrophe, *non?*'

He stared at her.

'Besides, it's man-made.' She smoothed her hands over the gentle swell of her hips, drawing attention to the obvious fact that *she* wasn't.

'Nice move, doll,' he drawled, following the movement of her hands. 'You're very pretty, and I'm sure you've got men lining up down the drive, but conscienceless women do nothing for me.'

Her hands stilled on her hips. She looked slightly shocked, and for a moment he wondered if it was another ploy, then she lifted her chin and said coolly, 'Perhaps you can get the parts and fix it?'

He could fix it?

Despite his irritation Nash almost laughed. Was she serious?

'Yeah, that easy,' he drawled, losing his battle not to pay too much attention to her silk nightgown, or something resembling one, and its faithful adherence to the lines of her body.

In particular when she moved—as she was doing now—it became highly revealing. The silk clung to the long, slender length of her legs, the jut of streamlined hips and the delicate curve of her clearly braless breasts. His body shifted up to speed. She rivalled the Bugatti in terms of fine lines.

He'd lied. She *did* do something for him.

'Looking for something?' Her voice was suddenly sharp, and it had lost its sleepy sexiness.

Nash dragged his gaze from the view to find those amber eyes observing him rather shrewdly. She'd clearly ditched the princess-without-a-clue act.

'Yeah,' he responded dryly. 'A conscience.'

She folded her arms, as if discovering some long-lost modesty.

'Oh, it's there,' she drawled, 'you just have to rattle around for it a bit.'

It was one hell of a line.

Against Nash's will a smile ghosted across his mouth. Not such a dumb blonde after all.

'I'll take a pass.'

'Shame.' This was said with a little toss of those curls as she walked towards the scene of her crime: the rear end of the Bugatti. 'But I'm sure it can be fixed. It's only tipped into some roses bushes after all—a little scratched paint at most.' She looked at him over her shoulder. 'Nothing to get all worked up about.'

Was it his heated imagination or in that moment did she drop her gaze infinitesimally below his belt?

He could hear one of his people speaking on the other end of the phone. He lifted it momentarily and said, 'Give us a minute, mate.'

'Have you changed your mind?' She paused deliberately—it could only be deliberate with this woman. 'About the car?'

'Nothing's changed, sweetheart, except your fine day.'

He watched the confidence dip slightly out of

her body, and oddly it didn't give him the satisfaction he would have anticipated.

'Expect a bill.'

She notched up her chin. 'Can I expect anything else?'

'Yeah—a lecture from your old man about why messing around with another guy's wheels can get you into all sorts of trouble.'

For a moment she looked at him as if she was going to say something about that, and for some reason he found he was hanging on her answer.

Instead she pushed back her tousled hair, gave him a distracted smile, as if she knew something he didn't, and headed back the way she'd come.

He wouldn't have been a red-blooded man if his gaze hadn't moved inexorably to what he had noticed before: a very shapely behind. It was like a perfect peach, all high and perky under the clinging silk of whatever it was she was wearing—or not wearing.

Vaguely he became aware that the old Italian bloke was glaring at him, and he dragged his eyes off the view.

'The car is not so damaged you need to frighten her,' grumbled the older man, 'and you can keep your eyes to yourself. Miss St James is a nice woman. She does not ask for all this trouble.'

Nash could hear the disembodied voice coming from his cell, but he was slightly bemused by the lecture being delivered to him in hot, angry Italian. Who *was* this guy? Her father?

'I know your type, with the flashy car. You want to find some loose woman, you go into town.'

Loose woman? What was this? 1955?

'No, mate, I just want the car. Fixed.'

He was tempted to gun the Veyron and leave the Bugatti to its fate. But it went against the few principles he had left. The old girl was a treasure, and she deserved to be treated like the lady she was.

He settled the pick-up details and was strolling over to the Veyron when he was distracted by the very distinctive sound of high heels hitting flagstones.

'Miss St James' had re-emerged in silky white pants, which were swishing around her long legs, some sort of floaty, shimmery silky green top, which barely skimmed the tops of her arms and left her shoulders bare, and she'd applied bright crimson lipstick to that smart mouth of hers. Although her eyes were impenetrable behind those ridiculously large sunglasses she had a faint smile on her lips as she headed over to a boat of a convertible parked by the garden wall. He watched her climb in.

He was done here. He still wanted the car, and he wanted it fixed. But first he'd deal with the thorny question of *why* the Bugatti was nose-down in a bunch of roses.

'Hold it, sweetheart.'

She paused from rummaging in her bag, pointed chin angled over her shoulder, shades lowered, eyes assessing. 'Is there something else?' she enquired civilly.

Yeah, too civil.

He knew how to get his point across—how to use leashed aggression as a weapon in the male-dominated industry in which he'd shouldered his way up to the top.

He was somewhat stymied by the fact that as he approached the car she smiled, and her whole face softened, became sensuously lovely, almost expectant.

'Before you rip out of here,' he drawled, leaning in, 'just a word of advice.'

'Advice?'

'Lawyer up.'

Her smile flickered and faded. But before he could read her expression she pushed the shades abruptly up her face.

'As much as I like being tumbled out of bed by a handsome man and lectured to,' she shot out rapidly, her words scrambling over one another, 'I *do* have an appointment and this is all getting rather complicated.' She gave him a haughty look. 'If there is any damage to the car, add it to the bill, why don't you?' She zipped up her bag and muttered something about it being just one more thing to add to the list.

She wasn't stupid, Nash thought, looking down at all those bright pretty curls, but her sense of self-preservation was clearly running on zero. Didn't she realise if she was a man he would have hauled her out of that car and done what was necessary?

Maybe she did. Maybe she was relying on her woman status to keep her out of harm's way.

He reached in and palmed her keys.

'Hey!'

He levelled her with a look and had the satisfaction of seeing her back up in her seat.

'Yeah, about that. The world doesn't run on your timetable, princess.'

Her expression was hidden behind those shades, but the pulse at the base of her slender throat was pounding and the old bloke's accusation about her being a nice woman and him frightening her returned full strength.

He dropped the keys into her lap.

'Just as a matter of interest—mine, not yours, doll—how *did* the car end up in the garden?'

She fumbled to start her engine and he frowned. He wanted her to understand the consequences of her carelessness, but he didn't bully women.

She started up the engine, not looking at him.

'I think that would be when I left the handbrake off,' she responded, and without another word reversed fast in a cloud of dust.

Douleur bonne, what did she think she was doing?

Lorelei held on tight to the wheel as she tore up the drive, her heart pounding out of her chest. She just had to get away before the handsome stranger wrecked everything.

Alors, she could have just offered up a standard apology and volunteered to pay for all repairs. A more prudent woman would have done just that. But prudence wasn't her forte lately…

She just wanted today to be a nice day.

One more day.

Was it too much to ask?

She licked her dry lips, dragged her bag over as she drove, fumbled for her lipstick.

Don't think about it, she told herself, swiping her lower lip with the crimson colour, making a mess of it.

She braked, dropped the lipstick, fished it from her lap and hooked off her sunglasses impatiently to restore her face with a tissue in the rear-vision mirror.

For a moment all she saw were her eyes, huge and dilated and vulnerable.

Taking a deep breath, she put herself back in order and forged onto the highway, determined to put this behind her. *Oui,* she'd had a bad start to the day, but that didn't mean anything, and it wasn't *that* bad. Despite the trembling of her hands on the wheel she'd had a little fun, hadn't she? She was sorry about the car, but it hadn't been intentional and it was only a little scratched. She was a good person, she'd never hurt anyone on purpose in her life, she wasn't careless with other people's property; she wasn't a criminal...

Her heart had started pounding again.

Best not to think about it.

She depressed the accelerator, the wind tugging at her hair. Perhaps if she drove a little harder it would help.

She was living harder, too. She'd really pushed the boat out last night. In fact thinking about it made her feel a little sick.

She had positively, absolutely drunk too much. She'd flirted with the wrong men and her attention had definitely not been on her borrowed adornment for the twenties-themed party. When someone had pointed out a couple of the younger partygoers, climbing all over it, she had moved it herself, parking the vehicle in the private courtyard. Clearly she hadn't put the handbrake on.

Why hadn't she remembered to put the handbrake on?

For that matter, why had she behaved so poorly this morning? Why hadn't she apologised and done her best to smooth things over? Perhaps the better question was, what was she trying to prove? Was she that desperate for attention? For somebody to realise she needed help?

Brought up short by the thought, Lorelei let her foot retreat from the accelerator.

Did she need help?

The notion buzzed just out of focus. Certainly she wouldn't be asking any of her friends, none of whom had offered even a word of sensible advice since this whole nightmare began. Could she even call any of those people at her home last night friends? Probably not.

It didn't matter. At the end of the day a party merely meant she wasn't alone. She hated being alone. You couldn't hide when you were alone…

In the rear vision mirror she caught a flash of red. Instinctively she depressed the accelerator. The car did nothing. She tried again and realised she was pumping her foot. Panicking slightly, although this had happened before, she gently stood on the brakes, bringing the car to a slow standstill on the roadside. She saw the sports car flash past in a blur of red and ignored the pinch in her chest because he hadn't even slowed down. Not that she could blame him.

Had she really expected him to stop?

There was nothing for it but to turn off the engine for five minutes before taking it easy going down into town. The Sunbeam Alpine had been playing up for weeks. This wasn't the first time it had happened, and it wouldn't be the last.

Laying her elbow on the door and pressing her head against her hand, she closed her eyes, allowing the sun on her face to soothe the surging anxiety that threatened to sweep everything before it.

Nash watched the Sunbeam drop speed, weave a little. The brake lights stayed on as it ground to a standstill in a cloud of dust at the roadside.

He sped past.

He didn't have time for this. For any of it. The banged-up car, the performance in the courtyard...the unreasonable desire to pull over, pluck those shades off her eyes and rattle around for that conscience of hers she'd assured him she had.

He only got a few hundred metres down the road before he was doing a screeching circle and slowly heading back.

She hadn't got out of the car She seemed to be just sitting there.

Nash already wanted to shake her.

He pulled the Veyron in behind and killed the engine. Shoving his aviators back through his thick brown hair, he advanced on her car. Still she hadn't shifted.

What did she expect? A valet service?

She was sitting with her head thrown back, as if the sun on her face was a sensual experience, her expression virtually obscured by those ridiculously large sunglasses. He noticed for the first time that she had a dappling of freckles over her bare shoulders. They seemed oddly girlish on such a sophisticated woman. He liked them.

His tread crunched on the gravel but she didn't shift an inch.

'Car trouble?'

She slowly lowered the glasses and angled up her face.

'What do you think?'

Those amber-brown eyes of hers locked on his.

'What I think is you need a few lessons in driving and personal responsibility.'

A smile, soft and subtle, drifted around the corners of her mouth. 'Really? And are you the man to give them to me?'

Nash almost returned the smile. She really was playing this out to the last gasp.

'How about getting out of the car?'

She gave him a speculative look and then slowly

began unhooking her seatbelt. Her movements were slow, deliberate. She unlatched the door, hesitated only for a moment and then swung her long legs out. She shut the door with a click behind her and leaned back against it.

'How can I help you, Officer?'

The scent of her hit him, swarmed through his senses like a hive of pretty bees, all honey and flowers and female.

Expensive, a steadying voice intervened. *She smells and looks expensive.*

Like any other rich girl on this coast. A dime a dozen if you'd got a spare billion in the bank.

He folded his arms. 'Going to tell me what's going on?'

He actually saw the moment the flirtatious persona fell away.

She gave a little shrug. 'There seems to be a problem with the engine. I accelerate but I lose speed.'

He nodded and headed for the front of her car.

Lorelei found herself following him, hands on her hips. He got the bonnet up with no trouble— something she never could. He leaned in.

'It's the original,' he told her in that deep, male voice.

'Are you a mechanic?'

'Near enough.'

Lorelei looked down the road as a couple of cars swished past, then back at the man leaning into the business end of her car.

Her eyes dwelt on the tail of an intricate dragon tattoo running down his flexed left arm, on his muscled shoulders, shifting under the fit of his close-weave black T-shirt, broad and imposing as he bent low, drawing attention to the strong, lean length of his torso and tapering to a hall-of-fame behind—all muscle. Prime male.

She snagged her bottom lip contemplatively, stroking him up and down with her eyes. She couldn't get over how thick and silky his dark brown hair looked, the wavy ends caressing his broad neck. She wondered how they would feel tangled between her fingers. She wondered what he would say if she apologised, if she told him she wasn't always this out of control…

'Whoever looks after it deserves a medal.'

Lorelei wondered a little hopelessly if he was ever going to look up—look at *her*. She gave a little inner sigh. Probably not. She'd burnt her bridges with this man.

'What was it?' he prompted. 'A gift?' When

she didn't reply he straightened up and gave her a speculative look. 'I'd say from a guy who knows his engines.'

Lorelei cleared her throat, aware she'd been staring at him and that he was probably aware of it. 'I bought it myself. At auction.'

He looked so sceptical her hands twitched all over again on her hips.

'You need a specialist to run some tests on the engine.' He was looking at her steadily, as if he expected her to be writing this down. 'It's in good nick, so I assume you've got a special-ist mechanic.'

She found herself recalled to her usual good sense. '*Oui.* I'll call him.'

'Everything else looks to be in order.'

As he spoke he set the bonnet down carefully, checked it was locked in place. His movements were assured and methodical and, oddly, Lorelei felt soothed by them. He treated her car with re-spect. Which was more than she had done with his employer's Bugatti, a little voice of con-science niggled.

'What will happen with the Bugatti?' she found herself asking.

'I expect the man who owns her will have some questions for you.'

Lorelei shoulders subsided.

'Do you want me to follow you back?'

No, most definitely not. Because she wasn't going back. She'd been running the Sunbeam like this for weeks, but she got the impression her handsome stranger would not be best pleased. He might not think much of her, but he was clearly in love with her car.

'*Mais non.* You stopped.' She pushed back a rogue curl dangling over the left side of her face. 'It's more than most people would have done. *Merci beaucoup.*'

Nash hesitated. He hadn't seen her like this before—calm, almost subdued—and it suited her. She wasn't quite as young as he'd first assumed—maybe thirty—and there was a maturity about her that he'd missed in all the glamour-girl theatrics.

'Right. Take care of her. She's a beauty.'

He ran his hand lightly over the paintwork and for the life of him couldn't work out why getting back into his car was so hard. Except she was just standing there, looking a little uncertain.

He sat in the Veyron, waiting, watching as she

climbed into the sapphire-blue roadster, waiting for her to start the engine, waiting for her to pull out, all the while waiting to feel relief that she was off his hands. She gave him a simple wave and drove slowly back down the road.

Telling himself he was satisfied, he pulled out and took off.

Lorelei watched until she couldn't see him any more in her mirror, then ignored the pinch in her chest because she wasn't going to see him again, before turning the big car around and heading back the way he was going. Into town.

CHAPTER FOUR

'LORELEI, good morning.' The girl behind the desk beamed. 'You're early!'

'No, I have a client at midday, so I'm running late, *chère*. Can you be an angel and put a call through to the arena to let them know I'm on my way?'

As she reached her locker Lorelei finished keying her successful morning's tally into her cell: *Smashed up a Bugatti. Met a man.* Then she hesitated, because 'met a man' implied she would be meeting him again. Monaco was a postage stamp of geography, but person per square foot it was the most densely populated postage stamp in the world, making it highly unlikely...

She sighed, pressed Send to her best friend's number and dropped the cell into her bag, placing that in her locker. Her love life was fairly, well, non-existent these days. Getting close to a man in her current situation just meant another person to hide things from.

She stripped, pulled on jodhpurs and a white shirt, and crouched down to yank on her riding boots. It was only when she stood up to don the regulation jacket and caught sight of her reflection that she paused to enjoy the little moment when she stepped into this world.

It was almost a moment of relief. She understood this world. There were rules and regulations and they were satisfying. It was what she had always loved about dressage and showjumping. She had had so little structure growing up, and the sport had provided for the lack. Ironically it was fulfilling the same function now.

She smiled wanly as she buttoned herself up. The jacket hung a little on her, but so did everything. She'd lost weight during her father's trial and somehow never regained it.

Gathering up her clipboard, Lorelei made her way out into the stands to wait for her student.

Once this had been her dream, until a bad fall had put paid to her ambitions. Nowadays she trained up-and-coming equestrians on a freelance basis. It didn't pay spectacularly well, but it was work for her soul. After the accident she hadn't thought she would ever saddle up again. Two years of rehabilitation had taught her both patience and determination, and she brought them to her work. It made her a good trainer.

In a couple of years, when she was financially back on her feet again, she hoped to set up her own stables on a property she had her eye on outside Nice. For now, she trained and kept two horses at the nearby Allard Stables, where she also volunteered.

She brought her focus to bear as a glorious bay gelding entered the arena, carrying a long-legged teenager. Lorelei had been working with her for a month. She watched as horse and rider trotted round the perimeter and then came out of the circle, performing a shoulder-in. Her practised gaze narrowed. The rider was using the inside rein to create the bend, rather than her leg, and was pulling the horse off-track.

Too much neck-bend, no angle, she noted on the clipboard propped up on one knee.

Some of the best equine flesh in the world was on view here most days, ridden by the best of the best, but on Fridays the arena belonged to students such as young Gina, who was making a hash of the most fundamental lesson in advanced dressage. She would improve—Lorelei was confident on her behalf. These were skills that could be learnt. The rest was about your relationship with the horse, and Gina was a natural.

For the next half hour she took notes, then joined Gina and the bay gelding's regular handler in the arena. She was working with Gina on top of her usual student load as a favour to another trainer, but she didn't mind taking on the extra work. It was good to take her head out of her financial troubles and focus on something she could control, and fulfilling to see the progress Gina had made in little over a month.

She worked with both girl and horse for the rest of their session, then joined Gina and her mother to talk about her progress. It was important, so although she was running late for her appointment at the Hotel de Paris she made the time. It was on half one when she leapt into the Sunbeam, starting her engine as she checked her cell.

It was never a pleasant experience. So many messages—so few people she actually wanted to talk to. There were several from her solicitor, a raft from legal firms she'd never heard of and one from the agent through whom she was leasing the villa out to strangers. She had a vague hope that the income could be channelled back into the upkeep of the house and grounds. But she wouldn't think about that right now. She wasn't ready.

Maybe tomorrow.

Unexpectedly the stranger's comment that she expected the world to run on her timetable flashed to mind. But before she had time to dwell unhappily on the truth of that, and aware that her damn hands were shaking again, she keyed in her best friend Simone's number and attached ear buds to enable her to drive and talk.

'You had a car accident? *Mon Dieu,* Lorelei, are you all right?'

'No, not an accident.' She hesitated, knowing how lame it was going to sound. 'I borrowed it for a theme party and parked it and left the hand-brake off.'

There was a pause before Simone said with a suspicion of laughter in her voice, 'You know I love you, Lorelei, but I would never let you drive my car.'

'Then perhaps you should talk to the guy I dealt with—this big Australian. He seemed to think I was a disaster waiting to happen.'

'Poor *bébé*. I'm sure you charmed him in the end.'

'He was a little steamed about the car.'

'I bet.'

'I don't think he liked me very much.'

Simone snorted. 'Men always like you, Lorelei. You wouldn't be so good at milking them of euros for that charity of yours if they didn't.'

Lorelei acknowledged the truth of this with a little shrug. 'I guess this one was the exception. He was different—I don't know…capable. Manly. He looked over my car.'

'And—?'

'I think I liked him.'

Simone was silent. Testimony to the state of Lorelei's romantic life.

'I know. I must be crazy, right?'

'Is he employed?'

'Oh, honestly.'

'The last one I heard about didn't have a sou to his name.'

'Rupert was an installation artist.'

'Is that what he called it? I know you're touchy about this, but for the life of me I can't work out why you don't date those guys you schmooze for your grandmother's charity.'

Lorelei's heart sank a little. The nature of her charity work meant she was often seen in social situations with powerful men, but she never dated them. Being the daughter of one of the most in-famous gigolos on the Riviera had left her wary of men who could pay her bills. She gravitated towards a type: struggling artist—whether it be painter or musician or poet—often in need of propping up, usually with *her* money. And that was where everything came unstuck.

Well, she didn't have that problem any more...

'So no name, no number—?'

'No hope,' finished Lorelei, and their laughter mingled over the old joke. 'I'm on my way as we speak to the Hotel de Paris.'

'*Ooh, la la,* tell me you're going to use their wonderful spa!'

'Not today. I'm being Antoinette St James's granddaughter and fronting for the foundation.'

'Your *grandmaman*'s charity?'

'*Oui.* They're doing a vintage car rally to raise funds for children with cancer. That's why I had the Bugatti on loan for last night's party. As an adjunct a racing driver here in Monaco has a pri-vate track a few miles inland, and he's going to run the kids around it for the day.'

'Which driver? Do you have a name?'

'I don't know. Let me see.' Lorelei braked at a pedestrian crossing and fumbled with the shiny folder she'd picked up from the Aviary office yesterday. 'Nash Blue. The name is vaguely familiar…'

The line went quiet.

'Simone?'

'I'm here. I'm just taking it in. Nash Blue. *Cherie,* how can you live in Monaco and not know anything about the Grand Prix?'

Lorelei rumpled her curls distractedly. 'I'm not very sporty, Simone.'

'You might want to keep quiet about that when you meet him.' Simone sounded arch. 'You didn't do *any* research, did you?'

'I haven't had time. It was dumped on me yesterday.'

'You *do* know Nash Blue is a racing legend?'

'Really?' Lorelei asked without interest, concentrating on weighting the folder down on the passenger seat with her handbag.

'He's a rock star of the racing world. He's broken all sorts of records. He retired a few years ago at the height of his career and—listen to this, *cherie*—he was earning close to fifty million a year. And I'm not talking euros. He was one of the highest paid sportsmen in the world.'

Must be nice, Lorelei thought vaguely.

'He gave up the track to design supercars—whatever *they* are. I think the consensus is he's some kind of genius. But, putting that aside for a moment, he's utterly gorgeous, Lorelei. I confess I'm a little envious.'

Unexpectedly Lorelei pictured a pair of intense blue eyes and wished she had this morning to do over again.

'I'm sure I'll do something to annoy him. I'm on a roll with that, Simone.'

'He rarely gives interviews. The few times he has he's been famously monosyllabic.'

Lorelei's heart sank. So she was going to have to do all the talking?

'But be *en garde, cherie.* He has a reputation with the ladies.'

'Oh, please. If he doesn't talk how does that even work?'

'I don't think much talking is involved.'

Lorelei rolled her eyes. 'I think I'm quite safe, Simone. You forget—I grew up watching Raymond ply his trade. I have no illusions left.'

'Not all men are rascals, *cherie.*'

'No, you married the one who wasn't.' It was said fondly. Lorelei found solace in Simone's happy marriage, her family life. But it wasn't something she ever envisaged for herself. Apart from Simone, her longest relationship had been with her twelve-year-old horses.

'All I'm saying is Nash Blue was a bit of a player in his racing days, and given his profile I doubt anything has changed.'

'*Oui, oui.* I'll keep that in mind.'

'All the parties and famous people you meet— you are one lucky girl, *cherie.*' Simone sounded quite wistful.

'I guess.'

And now she was lying to her best friend.

For a glancing moment Lorelei wanted to tell Simone about all the unreturned phone calls, the unopened emails…

But she couldn't tell her. She was so ashamed she had let it get to this point.

The villa was a money pit she couldn't afford to keep up, and the charity was an ongoing responsibility that took time away from paid work. Her father's legal fees and creditors had basically stripped her of everything else.

She'd lost so much in the last two years, first Grandy to illness and then her faith in Raymond. Right now the only thing that felt certain in her world was the home she had grown up in, and she was holding on to it by the skin of her teeth.

'Keep me updated, *cherie*.'

'*Absolutement. Je t'aime.*'

Lorelei was still thinking about the call as she turned into the Place du Casino and began thinking about where she was going to leave her car. She was running late, and thoughts of what awaited her at home were proving a distraction despite her best efforts to pretend to the contrary. Yet the sun was shining, which lifted her spirits, and she told herself she deserved to cut herself a little slack. Tomorrow she'd deal with all those intrusive emails. She might even front up at her solicitor's office—although perhaps that was going overboard.

She stilled as she caught sight of a familiar red Veyron parked right outside the hotel entrance. Brakes squealing, she came to a standstill midtraffic. The adrenalin levels spiked in her body, but it wasn't anything to do with thoughts of bills and creditors. Her heart pounded.

Behind her horns blared. She made a wide go-around-me gesture with her arm, scanning for a spot. She found one and cut across the flow of traffic, wincing at the blare of horns, but it was

worth it to back up into the nice wide space. Perfect. All she needed now was to hand over the
folder, smile at the racing-car driver and then
she could go and find her stranger and apologise, offer to buy him a drink or two and hope
her charm would do the trick.

She reapplied her lipstick with a steady hand,
unravelled the blue scarf she wore to protect her
hair from the wind and stepped out onto the road.

This time a car horn gave an appreciative little
beep as she sashayed across the Place du Casino
towards the maharajah's jewel box that was the
hotel. That was more like it.

The day was looking up.

He was late.

Nash didn't give it much thought. The publicist would wait. Cullinan would wait. Everyone
waited. It was one of the few useful by-products
of fame and perversely frustrating. Nash was
only too aware of the contradiction. It would be
interesting if for once he was stood up.

But another benefit was being able to help out
where he could for a worthy cause, and a kids'
cancer charity was pretty high on that list.

That was why he had ridden down from the

top floor in the middle of negotiations and now strolled across the lobby into Le Bar Américain. Five minutes of face-time and this charity rep would be keen to get going, given he'd held her up for…Nash glanced at his watch…thirty-five minutes.

He scanned the downlit warm ambience of the bar. John Cullinan was on a stool, leaning into both drink and cell as he cut some throats. He was the best in the business at what he did—as he should be, given what he was paid, Nash reflected. But you got what you paid for. Cullinan was worth every penny.

He killed the call the second he saw Nash. 'She's a no-show.'

Nash shrugged. It was of no importance, just a formality.

'I'll get onto the foundation—'

'Just forward the details to the guys at the track and let me know a time and we'll give the kids something to smile about.'

He was about to move off when he saw her. She had paused in the doorway to speak to the maître d'. Her head was slightly bent, exposing the lovely length of her neck and making those bare shoulders look impossibly seductive. He hadn't stopped thinking about those delicately boned shoulders, the fine stemmed length of her throat ever since he'd left her up on the highway.

Nash found himself unable to look away.

Was she meeting someone here? For some reason the muscles tightened all through his body as he cast an inclusive once-over across the room, hunting down the guy. No one had moved towards her, although she had pulled a lot of attention, and he knew in that instant she was alone.

For the first time since he'd quit racing professionally Nash felt the same competitive tension he'd used to before a race.

She turned to look across the room, pushing back a rogue curl with that gesture he remembered, and her eyes met his.

Even at this distance he could see her bow lips tighten. She didn't look happy to see him.

Irritation sparked as a dozen reasons why he should walk on by and forget about her waved themselves like red flags. Yet as every male head in the room turned as she headed his way he knew he wasn't going anywhere.

Lorelei found herself unable to look away.

He stood by the bar, stripped to a crisp white

shirt stylishly taut along his torso and dark tailored trousers. His shoulders were impossibly broad, and he radiated confidence and money and power.

Lorelei removed her sunglasses and just stood there, trying to make the connection.

But even as she turned to the maître d' and gave his name she knew what the answer would be.

A shiver ran through her. In this setting it was obvious he was the most powerful man in the room. He was certainly the most attractive, and the chasm between mechanic and the man standing before her was immense. It couldn't be leapt.

She'd been had.

Lorelei stiffened as his gaze landed on her.

She'd also been seen.

His eyes locked onto her and for a moment he looked as poleaxed as she felt. Then he frowned.

She straightened, determined that not by an inflection in her voice or the blink of an eyelash should he see how angry she was—although she wasn't quite sure with who, nor how foolish she felt. She headed over.

Men were looking at her. Men always looked at her. She was tall and blonde and for some guys she was a prize. What they didn't know was that she wasn't available to be won.

She did the prize-keeping and the awarding.

'Mr Blue, I presume?' She offered her hand unsmilingly.

He wasn't smiling either, but he took her extended hand with common courtesy.

Lorelei told herself to relax. So they'd had a little moment this morning? He was a professional and she was…well, volunteering her time. Surely this could be polite and…oh…

His hand closed around hers, warm and dry and secure, and she melted just a little behind the knees. Was he holding on a little longer than necessary? Lorelei felt the colour mounting her cheeks. As he released her hand his thumb shifted and gently brushed over the hardened skin at the base of her palm.

A faint look of surprise lit those blue eyes and Lorelei snatched her hand back, feeling exposed. She could hear her grandmother's voice. 'Lorelei, a lady is known by the softness of her hands.'

Silly, old-fashioned, not true, and yet…

Another man stepped between them. 'You'll deal with *me,* Miss…St James.' He read her name off an email printout that Lorelei could clearly see had the Aviary Foundation's logo.

Lorelei wanted to take a step back but she held her ground. She knew a cut-them-down-to-size gesture when she was on the receiving end of one. She'd experienced enough of them over the weeks when she'd attended her father's trial in Paris. Nobody wanted her to be the unrattled loyal daughter, especially the media, but that was exactly what she had been. Even if it had meant sitting in the shower every night, crying her heart out.

'Lorelei St James,' she said coolly, drawing on the self-control she had perfected during that awful period. 'Let me guess—you must be Mr Cullinan, the *delightful* man who spoke to our foundation's receptionist yesterday and left her in tears.'

The guy bristled, but Nash's cool, deep voice brushed him aside.

'It goes with the territory, Ms St James. Sometimes John doesn't know when to turn it off. Do you have paperwork?'

A little thrown by finding herself under the intent scrutiny of those blue eyes again, for a moment Lorelei had to think. *What paperwork?*

Then she pulled herself together and unclasped her handbag, producing the small glossy folder. Nash handed it over, sight unseen, to the scowling Cullinan.

'You can go, John. I'll handle this.'

Lorelei tried not to appear startled.

'Don't you want to discuss it?' She indicated the folder being carried away by Mr Cullinan. The foundation's president had been very clear: she was expected to go over the schedule with Blue's management.

'No,' he said simply.

To the point. Direct. Like any woman, Lorelei liked decisiveness in a man, but it also left her on the back foot. He'd taken away her reason for being here in a single gesture.

Now they were alone she felt even more exposed. Would he think she had some hand in this? That she'd known exactly who she'd been dealing with up at the house?

She decided to come right to the point. 'Mr Blue, was there a reason why you didn't introduce yourself this morning?'

Although she already knew the answer...

'At the time names didn't seem relevant.' His

eyes moved with interest over her face. 'And it's Nash.'

Because he wasn't going to be seeing her again. Lorelei remembered how obvious she had made her interest in him and found herself cringing. What was it he'd said about not wanting to discuss it? *He can't make it any more clear, Lorelei,* a little voice of self-preservation whispered. *He's not interested. He's seen you at your worst. Nobody wants to be around that...*

She was pulled up short. What was that he'd said about calling him Nash?

'Tell me, Ms St James, have you eaten?'

Suddenly they seemed to be standing so close. Certainly too close for her to think clearly. His blue eyes moved broodingly over her. Lorelei could feel her body actually quivering in response.

'Are you offering to feed me, Mr Blue?'

A look of amusement flickered unmistakably in those intense blue eyes. 'It would seem that way.' He indicated the bar. 'What's your poison?'

Fortunately the answer to that question was always there, even as she scrambled to process the fact he was asking her to lunch with him.

He murmured, 'Champagne cocktail,' to the

bartender and then quite casually slid his broad hand around her bare elbow.

His touch sent a shiver through her erogenous zones and Lorelei found she was wobbling a little on her heels as he began to walk her out of the bar.

'Should I ask where we're going?' Was that appallingly breathless sound her own voice?

His mouth twitched. 'Why ruin the surprise?'

It was silly to feel trepidatious but their history had been a little rocky today, and that hand on her elbow was a tad possessive for their short acquaintance. He was a take-charge guy, but she was a little apprehensive about what form that might take. She told herself not to be silly. After all, he was hardly going to throw her into a river with crocodiles. Was he? She'd scratched a car he clearly valued, and she'd apologised for that. *Had* she apologised?

Lorelei glanced up at him. He wasn't smiling, but she had yet to see him smile. Other guests and patrons were staring at them but Nash appeared oblivious. Simone's phrase...*a rock star of the racing world*...bumped into her consciousness. She was with a famous man. She guessed he was used to being stared at. Except the Hotel de Paris wasn't a place people usually stared…

For the first time in her life Lorelei realised *she* wasn't the main event.

The man she was with was.

He led her into the Jardin restaurant. It was impossible just to walk in and get a table—she'd tried once or twice before—but Nash did just that. As he seated her at the best table on the terrace, with the Mediterranean as a backdrop, her cocktail arrived. Hand delivered by the bartender.

This was a new experience.

'Merci,' she murmured.

A menu was placed into her hands and a waiter hovered as Nash chose the wine.

French sparkling.

How did he know?

Lorelei glanced at her cocktail and smiled a little at her own foolishness.

Mon Dieu, she was being positively girlish. Anyone would think she'd never sat down across from…a rock star.

She met those intense blue eyes and time trickled to a stop. She knew that look in his eyes. He hadn't looked at her that way when she'd been playing out her theatrics this morning—or perhaps she'd been too self-absorbed to notice.

No, she would have noticed *this*.

He was looking at her as if she was worth his time.

A flutter of feminine satisfaction winged through her chest even as her ego reminded her she was worth any man's time.

But this man wasn't any man, and he was interested and making no secret of it.

She felt hot and tingly and aware of her body in ways she hadn't been in such a long time.

Then she remembered what Simone had said about him being a player and she stood on the brakes. She lifted the menu.

'Did you plan to have lunch with the charity's representative, Mr Blue?' she enquired, pleased that her voice continued to be cool and play-by-my-rules.

'It's Nash.' His voice was low and lazy, 'And no, Lori, it wasn't on the programme.'

'It's Lorelei.' She didn't lift her eyes from the menu she was pretending to read. 'And I wouldn't want to hold up your important day.'

There was a pause and from the corner of her

eye she caught the movement of his arm as he reached into his jacket. 'Excuse me one moment.'

She lowered the menu. He was keying a number on his cell.

'Luc, I won't be back.' His tone of voice was abrupt and to the point—nothing like the easy male drawl he used with her. 'Have them send the contracts straight over to Blue. I'll deal with them tomorrow.'

Lorelei put the menu down.

He pocketed the cell.

'I take it that was for me,' she observed, lifting a finely arched brow.

The wine had arrived. He poured her a glass himself, then lifted his tall glass of sparkling wine and touched the flute in her hand.

He didn't smile, but his eyes caught and held the part of her fighting to get free, and in that instant Lorelei stopped struggling.

His voice was deep and affectingly roughened, as if coming from a part of himself he usually held in check.

'Consider me all yours for the afternoon.'

CHAPTER FIVE

WITH the Bugatti long dismissed from his mind as a fake and the over-the-top theatrics she had engaged in difficult to reconcile with the poised woman sitting opposite him, Nash found himself entertaining what would have seemed outrageous a mere couple of hours ago.

She was a huge distraction, but he would make the time.

As he had led her to their table he'd appreciated for the second time today the graceful dip of her long, slender back before it gave way to the small curve of her hips, and the subtle sway of those hips as she walked with ease on deathtrap heels. She possessed an innate old-style grace and a hint of athleticism he couldn't quite link up with the sybaritic lifestyle she seemed to embrace.

She intrigued him.

He hadn't been able to get her out of his head since he'd left her on the highway. In the past if he'd wanted something he'd gone after it. But this something had turned up at exactly the wrong moment.

In a week's time his re-entry into racing was going to hit the media like a virus. Everything he did would be scrutinized—the places he went, the parties he attended, the women on his arm. Crazy drama-queen blondes were not part of the package. He intended to keep a low profile and wait out the blood in the water period until the media moved on to the next high-profile sportsman and hounded *his* private life.

Any woman he was seen with now needed to be low-key, and preferably without her own media circus. He'd broken off an on again/off again sexual relationship with a well-known British actress earlier in the year for just that reason. He knew the press would dig something out and air it in the months to come, but he also knew she was soon going to be announcing her engagement and that should put paid to any rumours. He wanted his re-entry into the sport to be as low-key as possible—the opposite of the media circus he'd been caught up in during his twenties.

The woman sitting across from him was *exactly* what a PR team would order. Cool, classy, understated. Not that he had any interest in involving anyone else in his decision. This was between him and his libido…and the lovely Ms St James. Although he didn't intend to give her much say. Action, in his experience, was a far more direct method.

His gaze lingered on her uncovered shoulders.

There was something about the delicacy of her throat and collarbone and the quiver of those bare shoulders that made him think about her naked under a sheet.

'All mine?' She echoed his words. 'You should be careful what you promise, Nash.'

It was the first time she had used his name and her accent curled enticingly around it. His body tightened.

But those amber eyes were direct.

'Are you planning a long lunch?' she enquired sweetly.

Quiet amusement tugged at his mouth. 'Isn't that a requirement of your job description?'

'Pardon?'

'Public relations.'

She looked genuinely surprised. *'Mais, non,* I am not in public relations.'

He leaned back in his chair, enjoying looking at her, enjoying the game. After spending the last two hours fine-tuning contracts this was a nice reward. Lorelei was certainly easier on the eye.

'What do you call it, then?'

'A favour.'

He lifted a brow.

'I'm on the board of the Aviary Foundation,' she explained. 'The usual publicist broke her ankle and I was deputised as her stand-in.'

It fitted. Yet he was disappointed. The idea that she actually worked, held down a career, had weighted those glamorous blonde looks of hers in something concrete. He studied her fine boned face, looking for something else beyond the undeniable beauty.

'It's an influential charity,' he said finally. 'How did you get involved?'

'My *grandmaman* set up the foundation some years ago. I have her seat on the board.'

In other words she came from money. She hadn't lifted a pretty manicured fingertip to earn it. He glanced down at those hands, checked for a ring, then looked again. Her nails were unvarnished and worn down.

But a seat on the board? She'd merely stepped into the niche carved out for her. Broken nails aside, perhaps there wasn't anything here beyond the eyes and the smile and the sexy accent.

He shifted in his chair.

'Do you do a lot of charity work?'

'I do my share. If one is in a position to do so I think there's no excuse not to.'

'Agreed.'

'About this morning...' she said slowly.

He shook his head. 'I think we've moved on from that, don't you?'

Lorelei picked up her champagne and sipped it. Had they? She was grateful not to have to apologise or explain, because, really, how *did* she explain? She didn't want to look too closely at how out of control things had become.

He had that lazy, contented male look about him—as if he had her exactly where he wanted her and was sizing up his options with her. It was time to do a little sizing up of her own.

'I did some research on you,' she said, knowing it was only half a white lie—because couldn't Simone be counted as research?

He didn't look disturbed.

'You've got quite a reputation.'

Those blue eyes glimmered.

'As a competitor,' she added with a little smile.

He drummed the fingers of his left hand on the table. 'I don't like to lose.'

'It must make you hard to live with.'

'I wouldn't know.' He almost smiled. 'Not having to live with me.'

'I guess it's a question to ask your girlfriend—or wife.'

She didn't know why she'd phrased it that way. It was hardly subtle.

'There isn't a woman in my life.'

Lorelei knew she'd be a fool to believe that. Look at him—big, rugged, rich, sex appeal to burn.

'Oh, really? I heard you were quite busy in that department.'

'Did this come up in all that research?'

Lorelei ran her thumb over the stem of her glass. She realised he was watching her hand and that her gesture might be interpreted as quite provocative. She picked up her glass, intending to drink, then put it down again.

She'd had quite enough to drink last night.

'And you?' he prompted. 'Easy to live with?'

'Me?' She was no longer entirely sure what they were talking about. 'I'm a pussycat.'

'According to your husband?'

'No husband.' She met his eyes and saw satisfaction with her answer.

This time she did take a sip of her drink, and another.

She didn't get involved with men like this. Yet here she was, walking straight on in.

Whatever he said, he was probably seeing someone. Maybe not today, but certainly yesterday, and probably tomorrow. Girls were probably lining up around the block.

Her father in his heyday had always had two or three women on the go. One to pay the bills, another in reserve and a third he actually enjoyed sleeping with. Some young starlet or tourist passing through.

Lorelei frowned. She didn't like to think about that side of Raymond.

She preferred the side he'd thought she saw. He'd made an effort for her to see. The charming *bon vivant,* lavish with money and affection, especially with his darling daughter.

But she'd always been aware he romanced older women up and down the coast to keep the wolf from the door.

Her *grandmaman* had been the one with the real money, doled out sparingly.

Raymond had never complained, and his phone calls from the low-security prison where he was currently serving out the last months of a two-year gaol term were always full of jokes and cheer. She loved him for it, but she wished sometimes she could speak seriously to him.

She never had been able to breach that gleaming surface. Raymond didn't want to hear about the difficulties of life. And under the current circumstances she felt guilty even raising the subject of the villa.

Alors, she was back to thinking about the villa.

'Lorelei.' A deep voice said her name almost gently.

'Oui?' She blinked, took a breath.

Nash was watching her with an intensity that hadn't been there before, as if he knew something had changed.

'Sorry.' She made a forgetful gesture with one hand. 'You were saying?'

'Nothing that won't keep.'

He continued to watch her, a quiet smile conveying so much more than words. In that moment Lorelei knew she was in trouble.

Oh, she knew how to deflect a man, how to make it clear that despite sitting across from him, sharing a meal with him, she was not on the menu.

But right now she felt she was every dish he might like…

Finally Nash spoke.

'We've got a lot in common.' He settled back, angled in his chair, all shoulders and lean, muscular grace.

He seemed to be saying, *Take a good long look. It could all be yours.*

But for how long? she wondered.

'How do you gauge that?' she asked aloud.

'I like to compete. You're a serious trophy.'

'Pardon me?'

He gave her a lazy once-over she should have found insulting after the "trophy" description. Instead she felt it like a direct hit to her sleeping libido.

'You're smart and seriously sexy and I haven't been bored since I sat down with you. Like I said, you're a serious trophy.'

Lorelei inhaled sharply.

She knew this was how some men saw an attractive woman. She had just never met a man who had the nerve to say it to her in so many words.

'Nash, a trophy is an inanimate object you sit on a shelf.'

'A trophy can be anything you want to win,' he countered, sitting forward.

Lorelei had to remind herself not to edge back. He fairly emanated thumping male entitlement.

'I don't get in the race, Lorelei, unless I'm fairly confident of the outcome.'

For a breathless moment she considered asking him exactly how confident he was of her. But deep down she feared the answer.

Another Lorelei—the one who could hold men off with a death stare at a hundred paces—would have stood up and thrown the contents of her drink all over him. This Lorelei—the one clutching her glass like a life jacket and breathing in the spicy, earthy scent of him like oxygen—found herself asking, 'Is that a problem for you? Women boring you?'

He sat back, his hand resuming its drumming action. 'On occasion.' His head dropped a little to the side, as if he were considering her. He smiled slowly. 'Most of the time.'

Arrogant bastard.

She couldn't help smiling back.

'Perhaps the better question is, do you think you'll bore *me?*' she asked sweetly.

'How am I doing so far?'

Lorelei paused long enough to take another sip of her drink.

'Oh, I think you're in the race.'

Nash weighed up two options: dinner and dancing here in Monaco, or would he fly them to Paris? He was leaning towards the latter, because something about this woman made him want to impress her. She was beautiful, but she was also clearly highly intelligent…and wasn't that a turn-up for the books? He hadn't exaggerated when he'd told her he hadn't stopped thinking about her. But what if she hadn't turned up this afternoon? On the strength of her undeniable physical appeal would he have hunted her down? Until now he hadn't seen her like this—elegant, restrained…witty. Good company. Yet deep down he knew he would have gone looking, asked around, put in the legwork. There *had* been something about her from the beginning.

But this…the woman in full…was a revelation that made his body's unreasonable attraction to her no longer a betrayal of his common sense.

The chemistry between them was pretty much a flame to an oily rag, and if in the end she proved not much more than a spoilt rich girl it would be a disappointment, but it wouldn't stop him bedding her.

'Ms St James?'

Lorelei looked up. It was one of the waiters. She recognised him from the several other occasions she had dined here this year. He glanced nervously at Nash.

'I thought you should know your car is being towed away.'

'Pardon?'

'Your beautiful car, Ms St James. The authorities are taking it away.'

For a moment Lorelei didn't know what to do. Towed? Her lovely Sunbeam was being towed? But why…? This time she'd paid all the insurance and registration and…

She looked at Nash.

'I'm so sorry. I have to handle this.'

She scrambled to her feet, scooping up her handbag. Nash was getting to his feet too, frowning.

She wanted to see him again, but in that moment she knew it wouldn't work. She'd forgotten for a time just how bad things were for her out there. If circumstances were different in her world… But they weren't, and they seemed to be getting worse every day.

Without counting the cost of her actions, only knowing she would regret it if she didn't do it, Lorelei stepped up to him, put her hand gently to his jaw and lifted to kiss him. She inhaled man and aftershave, felt the heat of him and the surprising gentleness of his mouth because he hadn't expected this.

His momentary hesitation gave way to the sudden surge of his body against her own and his hand spread possessively across the back of her head. She tasted him fully as he moved to take over the kiss, giving her a moment's glimpse of exactly how overwhelming his sensual expertise could be.

Mon Dieu, this was what she was giving up…

But she was already pulling free, turning away, because she'd allowed herself to be seduced by the solidity and masculine certainty of this man when there was nothing here for her in the long run. All the while she was sitting here her problems were still out there, mounting up, waiting for her return, and now she had to deal once more with the chaos in her life.

She took off across the restaurant, as fast as her ridiculous heels would let her, knowing only one thing: she *had* to save the car. She wouldn't be letting anyone take away the last damn thing she owned.

Lorelei was across the Place du Casino and about to cross the road when a heavy hand curled possessively over her shoulder. She swung around, hitting out reflexively with her handbag, eyes wild with anxiety.

'Let me go. I've got to get to my car.'

Nash steadied her with both hands. 'I want you to wait here. Are you listening, Lorelei? Let me handle it.'

Responding to the authority in his voice, she blinked up at him. He was going to help? There was a scraping of metal on asphalt and, confused, she whirled around to see what was happening across the road. She saw the tow truck backing up in front of her car and automatically stepped out onto the road.

Nash swore and reached to grab her.

Of all the suicidal…

She took off across two lanes of traffic.

He wouldn't have believed it if he hadn't seen it, yet somehow she made it across unharmed.

His heartbeat slowly resumed normal strength.

Amidst the blare of car horns her high-decibel wishes were being made very clear in vitriolic French.

'Get away from my car!' she shrieked. 'What do you think you're doing?'

Nash was not often left speechless, but at that moment he might still have been in the court-yard at the old villa this morning. The sophisti-cated, sexy woman he had pushed back a busy afternoon's schedule for was gone. In her place was a reckless wild woman who was clearly out of control.

Adrenalin levels surging, he crossed the street more circumspectly, all the while watching as Lorelei stormed up to the guy supervising the removal of her car. She was waving her hands about as she remonstrated with him in typical Gallic fashion, but the guy was pretty much ig-noring her.

Hell, for all he knew they were on a first-name basis and that car of hers was towed every day of the week…

Lorelei had her hands on her hips and was gathering quite a crowd. Ice-queen blondes losing their cool on a lazy afternoon in Monte Carlo had pulling power, and now Lorelei was… Was she taking off her shoes? She was taking off her goddamned shoes! What in the hell?

She slung first one and then the other stiletto heel at the guy. The first one missed but the second one caught him in the groin.

The bloke said something crude and headed for her, and Nash dropped amusement and swapped it for street-level aggression. He made a direct line for the problem, collared the ape so fast the guy didn't see it coming and shoved him hard up against the side of the truck.

'You want someone to lay into, mate,' he said, low and with deadly menace, 'try me.'

The man's face fell, then turned an apoplectic red. Nash realised he had him in a chokehold. He eased off. But Lorelei was suddenly right up beside him, stabbing her slender index finger within inches of the guy's face.

'You listen to him and you listen to me. I want my car back. *Pronto!*'

Nash growled. 'Hand in my back pocket.'

'Quoi?'

'Keys,' he snarled.

Fumbling, Lorelei retrieved them.

'Get in my car.'

'But—'

'Do it. Now.'

She backed up, limped a little to the roadside, spotted the red Veyron across the street. She could only see one of her shoes. The other one seemed to have rolled under the truck. The red haze had shifted and she was beginning to think clearly again. What on earth had she done?

People were standing on the pavement, watching.

Let them watch, she thought miserably, casting a longing look back at her car…and then at Nash, who had let the guy go and was using his phone.

Possibly to call in the men with the straight-jacket for her before he made excuses to reverse right out of her life. She'd pretty much made a fool of herself, and from experience she knew that whilst men enjoyed the effort she put into her pretty packaging they didn't have much patience for her more high-octane behaviour. Not that she made a practice of causing scenes in public streets—no, that was a little more to do with the stress she was under at the moment. But Nash wasn't going to buy that. All he'd seen was crazy.

Serves you right, Lorelei St James, she thought as she picked her way across the road in bare feet.

She let herself into the car and forced herself to sit up dead straight, not slide down the seat and hide. She'd been doing enough hiding of late. It was an uncomfortable thought she quickly shoved out of her mind. But this was pretty bad. She'd behaved like a lunatic…

But, oh, her car.

Nobody would understand, but it was all she had left in her own name. It was the one thing she hadn't sold off to pay all the creditors. It was ridiculous, running a gas-guzzling monster like that, but when she drove it she felt like a queen in her castle—important, invincible…

All the things she had discovered recently she wasn't.

She watched Nash coming across the road. He looked so calm and in control. More things she wasn't.

He slid in alongside her, slamming the door, belting up, checking the lights as he fired up the quiet engine.

Lorelei fumbled for her cell.

'You don't need to make a call.'

She forced herself to look at him. Stupidly, her

eyes went to his mouth and she relived the moment she had impulsively kissed him. '*Au contraire.* I need to track my car. They'll impound it, and last time it took over a week to get it back.'

'Last time?' His eyes flicked over her.

Lorelei assumed a facsimile of a haughty expression but her heart just wasn't in it.

'I admit it has happened before,' she said wearily.

He didn't respond.

'It's such a large car,' she found herself explaining. 'I find it difficult to park.'

'You parked in a loading zone,' he inserted dryly.

Lorelei worked some invisible creases out of her silken lap. 'Yes, perhaps. I'm a little short-sighted when it comes to parking. It does happen.'

'Yeah, to you I'm guessing a lot.'

Lorelei didn't answer. What could she say? *Oui, I'm a mess on heels.* Oh, her Louboutins. Could she ask him to…?

She glanced sidewards. *Non*…

'Nash,' she said slowly, 'could you be a darling and fetch my shoes…?'

He shifted around in the seat, his expression not encouraging.

'They're very expensive,' she murmured with a hopeful upwards look. Would it help if she fluttered her eyelashes? Showed him the receipt from the shop in Paris?

Without a word he swung the sports car out into the traffic and Lorelei shrieked as he did an abrupt U-turn. She grabbed her seat, holding on for dear life.

He braked with a screech.

'Don't move,' he uttered, punching open the door.

No, she wouldn't be doing that. Although she might just have lost a couple of years off her life…

He returned with both shoes, dropping them into her lap. He didn't even look at her, just pulled the Veyron into the light traffic and drove away from the scene of her crime. Lorelei craned her neck to try and work out what was going on with her car.

'You'll have it back in the morning,' he informed her abruptly.

She stared at him stupidly.

'It's not being impounded. A mechanic is going

to have a look at that stop-start engine of yours. They'll run it up to you tomorrow.'

Lorelei plucked at her shoes, too stunned even to check for damage.

'Merci,' she said inadequately, wondering how she was going to begin to apologise and thank him. It had been so long since someone had done something just for her.

But what did it mean? This went beyond some silly flirtatious nonsense about a race and a trophy and him being out to win. He'd just done something very nice for her, and she couldn't enjoy it because she knew she had probably put the kybosh on this going any further.

As if sensing her disquiet, he turned those stunning eyes momentarily in her direction.

'I'll run you home,' was all he said.

She forced herself to shrug.

'Comme vous le souhaitez.' As you wish.

CHAPTER SIX

COULD he be a darling and fetch her shoes...?

As the traffic eased to a halt at a pedestrian crossing Nash snapped and did the only thing a man in his circumstances could be expected to do, given the series of events, the surging adrenaline and hot blood being pushed through his body, and the proximity of this unpredictable wild creature he had somehow become involved with.

He leaned across, slid a hand around the back of Lorelei's head, meshing his fingers slightly in the silky weight of her hair and releasing more of the fragrance of honey and flowers he could fast become addicted to, angled her astonished face and took her tender mouth with his.

The faint hint of champagne still clung to her lips. The warm sweetness of her breath as she gasped and sighed and made a little moaning noise before kissing him back made him want more. The feel of her, the rise of her response beneath him, suddenly stirred a much more primal urge to take what belonged to him, what was his. To mark her. He'd only known her a handful of hours and yet he felt as if he'd been waiting much longer to kiss her.

He deepened the kiss, invaded her mouth, tasting her, driving into her. He told himself it was sexual chemistry; it would burn itself out fast enough. But right now…he wanted her. He couldn't get enough of her. Yeah, he'd fetched her shoes for her…she could wear them while he—

The blare of a car horn and Lorelei jerking in response had Nash releasing her. For a second he was caught in the headlights of her eyes, and the analogy of having something not quite tame within his grasp was suddenly very real.

Who was this woman?

'This isn't a good idea,' he imparted roughly.

'Non?'

Her rather unhappy interrogative took him by surprise and he almost smiled.

He couldn't believe what he was thinking. He needed to take her where she wanted to go and then forget the whole thing. He was damn lucky someone hadn't been filming the entire incident in the street—although that was a possibility, given the crowd she'd drawn.

She was running her fingers through her hair, rubbing the spot where he'd had his hand…

He was under time constraints. In a couple of weeks he'd be going into lockdown.

He had to be out of his mind…

But he could see her home.

She seemed to realise what she was doing and pulled her hands back into her lap. The gesture made him smile. Yeah, he could see her home.

For a breathless moment all Lorelei had been able to do was hold still, drowning under the skilled pressure of his lips, but she'd never been a passive woman and with a little moan she had kissed him back.

Apparently women who caused scenes in the street didn't scare all guys away. Well, not this guy, at least, whose mouth needed a contract for insurance purposes. Lorelei guessed not much would scare him. Confidence and certainty didn't seem to be a problem for Nash.

He hadn't even asked. He just took.

Lorelei was quite certain his not asking was adding to the outrageously good feelings still slip-sliding through her body. *Mon Dieu,* the man knew what to do with his mouth—and those fingers, lightly, firmly palpating the sensitive tendons and hollows at the top of her neck, tugging so pleasurably on her hair, were equally skilled. What could they do elsewhere on her body?

When his mouth had released hers she'd been panting slightly, and she hadn't been able to take her eyes off him as his gaze had drifted over her face, down across her bare shoulders.

'This isn't a good idea,' he'd said, in a flatteringly roughened voice.

A cold drop of uncertainty had hit the top of Lorelei's spine. *'Non?'*

He had smiled then, the charisma of it almost shocking. His blue eyes had filled her line of vision but the light honk of a horn had had her shaking off the spell and indicating vaguely at the windscreen.

'I think we can go.'

Nash moved lazily back to his side of the car, as if he had all the time in the world, and they shifted forwards, his hands on the gears as assured as they had been when splaying long, strong fingers through her hair. He hadn't pulled, like a less skilled man might. He'd tugged. And the little answering darts of response had shot like arrows from a quiver through her body.

She threaded her own fingers through her hair and then realised she was trying to recreate the feelings he'd evoked in her. She snatched her hand back, pressing it in her lap.

Feeling as if she might be slumping unattractively, Lorelei tried to sit up a little straighter, assume a more ladylike posture—only to find she was actually still upright. There had been no slippage…only a complete and utter inner landslide…

It was all about how she felt inside, she realized. All loose and relaxed and devil-may-care. The stake of anxiety she'd been tied to all day had gone. *Mon Dieu*—she ran an unsteady hand through her curls—the man was a miracle-worker. What on earth would it be like if…?

Nash gave her a slashing smile as if he understood exactly how it would be.

The courtyard was in full afternoon sun when the Veyron idled to a stop.

Nash killed the engine and without a word to her—not that they had exchanged many words driving up, at least not any important ones, as to what they were doing, if he'd be staying, where this was going—he was out of the car and coming around, lifting her door.

Lorelei tried to think fast. She was more than a little worried about inviting him inside. Most of the rooms in the villa were emptied of furniture, and the general air of neglect that hung over the place was worse on the inside. She hadn't minded having people in last night, with all the lights and champagne flowing and the rooms thick with people, but in the harsh light of day she knew how bad it looked. And after this morning's series of disasters she suddenly wanted Nash to think well of her.

But Nash wasn't paying any attention to the house.

He was looking down at her.

She hadn't quite appreciated just how big he was until this moment. She'd had a taste of it this morning, but in her heels some of the height discrepancy had been dealt with. Right now, Louboutins dangling from one hand, handbag from the other, she was only too aware of his powerful shoulders, the strength of his arms and how easily he could overpower her.

It was a jolting thought. Not that he had given

her any reason to think he was a threat to her safety—on the contrary. But she was a woman who lived alone and he was…

A famous man who was hardly going to turn into Jack the Ripper.

He shut the car door behind her. 'Shall we go inside?'

'*Ah, oui.* Of course.' She picked her way across the gravel, thinking there was no *of course* about it.

At the front door he held out his hand.

'Key?'

'It's open,' she said, struck by his old-fashioned attitude, and pushed open the heavy front door.

Nash shoved his hand against the panelling, holding it wide for her.

'Anyone else home?'

'*Non.* I live alone.'

His eyes found hers. They were so close she could see the unusual darker rim around the blue iris. Suddenly she knew why those eyes gave the impression of such an intense blue.

'You shouldn't live alone,' was all he said.

Her gaze dropped helplessly to the firm line of his mouth.

'That's why I throw a lot of parties.'

He didn't smile as she wanted him to. Nor did he kiss her. But she'd already worked out that Nash wasn't going to do much of what she wanted him to. He was his own man in ways she hadn't quite encountered before and it was in equal measures confusing and unbearably exciting.

His heavy tread rang out on the stone floor and the cool emptiness of the house closed in around them. Lorelei shivered slightly as her mood did its usual dip. Almost as if he was reading her, Nash stepped up behind her and she had an odd sensation of his strength and solidity. She rather liked it.

She liked it a lot. And all of a sudden she realised this man didn't feel like a threat to her. He was making her feel safe. And safety had been the most elusive of conditions in her life.

Her father had taught her to live with risk; her *grandmaman* had constantly moved the goalposts to keep her forever striving to do her best. Past boyfriends had relied on her to keep the wolf from the door with her inheritance, her network of social contacts.

None of them had ever made her feel safe.

It was probably illusory. He was a big, take-charge guy and he'd been sweet to her all along the line. No wonder she was having rescue fantasies.

She took him through to the kitchen. It was one of the few rooms still fully furnished, for which Lorelei was silently grateful. But unfortunately, like her bedroom, it was a shambles. The caterers had taken away most of their debris, but there were still empty bottles and plates and overturned furniture.

'I had a party last night,' she felt obliged to explain. She didn't want him to think she lived in squalor.

'I'm guessing that's pretty standard for you.'

It was. It was standard for her role with The Aviary. 'Not at all,' she replied smoothly. 'I'm quite the homebody.'

He gave her a sceptical look. 'Yeah, the party comes to you.'

Lorelei didn't know why but there was an edge to what Nash was saying that had her cooling. *He* should try entertaining eighty people on the budget The Aviary Foundation gave her.

Nash was surveying the room. He wandered over to the counter. Lorelei followed his long muscled back with her eyes.

'Coffee pot?'

'My, my—you are domestic.'

Nash shrugged. He had a housekeeping service at all his homes, which made it unnecessary for him to ever approach a kitchen, but he'd grown up regular. As regular as a kid with a drunk for a father and only an older brother to care for him. He'd learned young how to wash his own dishes and scrub a floor and unplug a drainpipe.

Not to mention how to get himself off to school.

'Yeah, I'm a regular boy scout.'

He looked around. Lorelei had a kitchen and a half. Although he doubted she ever spent any quality time with a dishmop.

Not a domestic bone in that lithe, lovely body, he thought with satisfaction.

Lorelei began opening cupboards, retrieving ground coffee beans, switching on the kettle, pulling out the coffee maker.

'Cups?' he asked.

Lorelei indicated one of the cupboards.

'You're very practised at this,' she said.

He appraised her. 'I know how to make a cup of coffee.'

'Your *maman* brought you up right.'

'Mum walked out when I was nine.'

Nash caught himself. *Where in the hell had that come from?*

Lorelei's gaze moved to his. 'Parents,' she said carefully. 'They do muck us up.'

'Yeah.'

Lorelei noticed he spoke matter-of-factly, but there were hard emotions playing over his face and she kept her attention on the job at hand.

Unavoidably, she began thinking about her own *maman*—Britt, who had flickered in and out of her life. The mother she'd only known fractionally as a child, on those rare visits to New York and her apartment high above Central Park. A glorious blonde Valkyrie who sang to her Swedish folk songs and let her play dress-up in the *ateliers* of the best couturiers in Paris and Rome; a mother of sorts, who'd stalked the catwalks with Lorelei sitting front and centre at the shows, dressed up like a little doll to be cooed over by her glamorous, sweet-smelling friends. A mother who had been no mother at all, and was now a sort of friend she spoke to irregularly.

'I gather someone in your family owns a bank, given the real estate you're sitting on.' Nash was leaning back against the counter, muscular arms folded across his chest, displaying the tail of the dragon tattoo down his left arm.

'Not a bank.' Lorelei repressed a wry smile. *If only.* 'This house belonged to my *grandpère.* He had a successful import business. When he died it passed to my *grandmaman,* Antoinette St James, and I inherited it on her death.'

'I gather you were close? She left you her house.'

Lorelei wanted to say, *It's complicated.* 'She looked after me. Taught me right from wrong. Gave me standards.'

'And a house?'

'Oui.' She sighed. A white elephant.

'I imagine it's a burden, given its size?'

He understood. It didn't surprise her as much as it ought. He gave the impression of being quietly observant. What had Simone said? Monosyllabic? She imagined this was as chatty as Nash got, and it was quite a compliment to her.

She gestured at the ceiling. 'You don't need to be kind. It's clearly falling down around my ears.'

She waited for him to ask her why she didn't sell it. It was the obvious question.

'Did you grow up here?'

'In part. I spent my breaks between school terms with Grandy.'

He nodded. He was examining her as if she were something he was thinking of buying. Lorelei took the burbling coffee jug over to the counter.

'I take it your parents are gone, given you got this house?'

'*Non,* both living. My *grandmaman* didn't quite approve of my mother.'

'But she approved of you?'

'*Ah, oui,* in her way. Cream? Sugar?'

'Black.'

'Raymond, my father, did not meet with her approval, either.'

'You call your dad by his given name?'

Lorelei gave a little Gallic shrug. 'He's that sort of father. What do you call your *papa?*'

'Not much. He's dead.'

'I'm sorry.'

He watched her pour. 'Don't be.'

'Do you have siblings?'

'An older brother.'

'That must be nice. I'm an only child. Are you close?'

He looked down at her. 'Want to trade family horror stories, Lorelei?'

She froze. For a moment she thought… But, no, he didn't know. He would have said something. Lorelei lowered her gaze. She didn't have anything to be ashamed of. She hadn't broken the law. She was a good person….

'I don't have any.' She spoke too quickly.

Nash watched a tide of faint pink colour move across the surface of her high tilting cheekbones. She suddenly looked a whole lot less certain of herself.

He wondered wryly when his decision to come inside and see where this led had turned into a download of family stories over coffee. Probably about the time she'd climbed out of the car outside and looked up at him with those uncertain eyes. For some reason what had flashed through his head was not an image of her naked on a bed upstairs in this shambles of a house, but a vision of her stepping in front of those two lanes of traffic and the two minutes it had taken off his life.

There was something about this girl that told him she didn't have much of a clue about looking after herself.

He suspected the little stunt in the street today

was the tip of the iceberg. It should be sending him in the opposite direction. With the media circus about to start up around him, his every move monitored, he'd be insane to bring something like this into his life, even for a night.

'Nash, is this your usual modus operandi with women?' she enquired, tipping up her chin, all signs of uncertainty gone. 'Rescue them, drive them home and get them drunk on coffee?'

She'd read his mind.

He'd be a busy boy for the next eight months and he wasn't looking for a long-term lover. He was looking for what most men wanted but didn't own up to: a hot blonde who disappeared in the morning. He remembered that over that restaurant table he'd seriously considered Lorelei might be that woman.

He considered it again.

She could make arrangements, pack an overnight bag. He'd sort the plane, show her the nightlife of Paris, acquaint himself with the sweet, sensual weight of what he'd held in his arms momentarily inside the restaurant…

He watched her sashay over to the kitchen table, prop that pert little ass of hers up on the distressed oak surface and dangle a long, lithe leg.

Caution be damned—why the hell not?

He'd suggest dinner, mention the restaurant, wait for her to pack a little bag.

She was sipping her coffee, twining a glossy curl around a finger, amber eyes busy on him. It might have been his imagination but she seemed to sit a little straighter, and those eyes grew a little warier the closer he came. Yeah, those eyes did all the speaking for her, and if he sensed a raft-load of secrets was lurking behind them it didn't concern him. He wasn't interested in uncovering her secrets. He just wanted to know what she was doing tonight.

He stopped in front of her.

'I've been giving tonight some thought.'

'*Ah, oui.*'

He'd actually been thinking about some fine dining at a famous first arrondissement hotel, but something a little more cutting edge might be a better setting for Lorelei.

'If you're not engaged?'

Lorelei put down her coffee. '*Mais, non.*'

He reached for her hands, turned them over in his. She let him.

'Dinner?'

'*Oui.*'

To his surprise her lashes swept down and for a moment she looked almost demure, rather old-fashioned.

'Paris?' He cleared his suddenly husky throat. 'There's a restaurant in the fifth arrondissement.' He named a legendary chef.

Her lashes swept up in surprise. 'Can you get a table at such short notice?'

He shrugged.

Lorelei was impressed. She'd forgotten. Not only did he have money to burn, he was famous. She wished he would stop stroking her hands. She didn't want him turning over her palms, finding those calluses again.

She also wished he hadn't said those words to her in the restaurant: *I don't get in the race if I'm not sure of the outcome.* Although forewarned was forearmed.

She tugged her hands away. 'I'm afraid not to-night, *non.* Not Paris.'

She didn't want to wake up tomorrow morning in a hotel room on her own, or with a man who had taken his fill and was only going to trans-port her home.

He had clearly set the tone of what this was all about for him. This was a race and she was the trophy. No doubt he'd collected a lot of trophies—possibly had a shelf for them, she thought snappishly.

Lorelei had no intention of sitting on a shelf. She had seen too much of it growing up with Raymond. Womanisers left her cold. If Nash wanted to pursue her, he was going to have to do just that.

No? Nash looked long and hard at that unexpected negative. *No?*

'Can I ask if it's personal, or Paris?'

'I'm fond of Paris,' she demurred. 'But not tonight.'

Nash regarded her bright curls, her glossy slightly parted lips, her guarded eyes watching him.

'I'd be happy to go to dinner with you here in Monaco,' she suggested slowly.

So much for the disappearing hot blonde.

He almost smiled. Almost.

For some reason he didn't really mind.

She had the brakes on. He could almost see the marks on the road.

He didn't have to think about it. Any intention he'd had of fast-forwarding this evening suddenly seemed crass, and in his mind's eye he'd already put it aside in favour of a long, slow build-up. Lorelei, clearly, would be worth it. Given the slightly haughty look on her face, she set a high value on herself—and who was he to argue with that?

'Monaco it is,' he said. 'I'll pick you up at eight.'

CHAPTER SEVEN

'THAT woman, she's got a media profile.'

John Cullinan's voice came stridently over the speakerphone.

Nash strolled naked across the bedroom of his penthouse apartment, towelling his hair dry.

He had left Lorelei's home only a few hours before and felt comfortable that he'd dealt with his unlooked-for attraction to her. He was old-style enough to appreciate her definite *No, not tonight, not Paris.* It showed her to be discriminating, which pleased him, but he was confident a few dates would suffice and she'd let him into her bed. It was the primary goal.

He liked to set goals.

At his non-response Cullinan continued, 'Her da's banged up in one of those low-security places out in the countryside. There was a celebrity trial a couple of years back. He defrauded a washed-up French actress out of her savings. But the star turn was the daughter. She turned up every day at the trial in a different outfit, stole the show. Seemed to enjoy the limelight.'

Nash threw down the towel and checked the time by his watch sitting on the bedside table.

'She doesn't even work for that goddamned charity.'

Nash stilled.

'Who doesn't work for the charity?' he asked, nice and low.

'Lorelei St James. And, get this: there's a string of high-profile men she's been linked to. That dot-com billionaire who dropped a fortune on the casino last year, a Hollywood producer, the financier Damiano Massena—pretty much any guy with a bit of a name and she's there. She targeted you today, boyo.'

Nash was caught off guard.

'You've got an overactive imagination, John.'

'Just doing my job. You can't afford the press. This woman likes the press.'

'Don't they all?' Nash muttered under his breath. 'The press conference is all you need to worry about, mate. Are we clear?'

'Clear.'

Nash cut the connection, running a hand through his damp hair.

He didn't want this information. But now he had it, what was he going to do with it?

There was one option, he thought. He didn't have to do anything about it. So she had a crim for an old man? Big deal. So did he. She had a past. Again, big deal. So did he. She was a beautiful grown-up woman who had lived in the world just like him, not a boring ingénue. Part of what attracted him to her was that life experience, her maturity.

It would be highly suspicious if she *didn't* have a past.

She had a past with *'a string of high-profile men.'*

He stood over his suit, laid out over the back of a chair—the suit he'd pictured Lorelei pressing her long, lithe body against, with him in it, as he danced with her, resting his hand on that sweet place at the bottom of her spine.

He laid that same hand on the back of his neck, where the tension seemed to be gathering at a rate of knots.

He pictured Lorelei in the arms of another man, and another. The woman in the backless gown remained the same, the suit was the same, but different guys. He frowned and dismissed it.

He reasoned that Cullinan didn't like her because she'd shown him up in the American Bar. The recollection of which had a bit of a smile tugging on his lips.

Relaxing, he retreated into the bathroom, palmed his electric razor and went to work on a beard that would be back in the morning.

Besides, if she was after some limelight wouldn't she have jumped at Paris?

How many media-savvy socialite blondes had he walked out of restaurants and into a posse of click-happy paparazzi who'd just *happened* to get a clue as to where he was dining and with whom?

He was accustomed to women with agendas. Years ago, when he'd still been green about the limelight, a young banking heiress had decided she wanted a racing-car driver. He'd been twenty-four, idealistic and he'd put a ring on her finger. Not an engagement ring—he hadn't been *that* naive—but he'd imagined that was what it took to assure her fidelity. She'd slept around on him from the beginning, and when they'd broken up she'd hit the media with the credentials of a seasoned campaigner.

It was the origin of all the stories about him. His heiress had turned him into a legend of infidelity, citing women he had never known. Her public profile had assured that she'd gone on to a career as consort to a series of high-profile men.

He'd gone on to a legendary driving career and a reputation for moving through women faster than he sped around any track. The media had been insatiable for stories about him. He had fed them with his policy of never lingering with one particular woman too long, there was no getting away from that, but he had never courted public attention. It had come after him, and consequently he had no illusions left about the negative side of publicity, about its effect on his attempts to lead a semi-normal life, and especially about the women who hustled their way into that life.

Yet here he was, deluding himself...

The razor dropped into the basin and he let it buzz there uselessly, leaning the heels of his hands on the sink and eyeing himself in the mirror.

Did he really need to give himself the lecture? At this stage in his life? Hadn't he already been here before?

If Cullinan was right, this was a woman who liked the limelight, who liked famous men, and she'd turned up at that hotel today and lied to his face that she had no idea who he was.

He vented a dry laugh. He'd been here so many times it was like a stuck record. In former days he would have just taken what was on offer and ignored the fallout. But he had more to protect this time around. Because right now, with his racing career once again poised in the wings, he was going to do things differently.

His expression hardened.

He knew what he had to do. He just didn't want to do it. But he couldn't in good conscience sleep with a woman and then dump her. He could be ruthless in his personal relationships, but he wasn't a bastard.

He snagged his cell before he could change his mind and put through a call.

She answered after several rings. *'Bonjour, Nash.'*

Her voice was lilting, husky…inviting him in.

For a second he forgot all his misgivings and he was back on the side of that highway, watching her standing uncertainly by her car. The difficulty he'd had in driving away…

Something about this wasn't familiar. None of this was familiar. This. Her.

No, he hadn't done this before…

Damn.

'I'm ringing to cancel,' he said bluntly.

There was a silence.

'It wasn't a good idea to begin with. I've got a lot of work on and I can't give you the time you deserve.' He knew these lines by heart. 'I apologise if I've messed up your evening's plans.'

He waited for the explosion. In his experience a woman on the make rarely remained neutral.

'You didn't know this earlier today?'

She didn't sound angry, she sounded genuinely at a loss, her voice almost uncertain, and for a moment it loosened his grip on all that life experience. He hesitated, because right now he was remembering he'd seen a lot of other things in Lorelei St James beneath the glossy exterior. Things he couldn't think about now or they'd undermine what was the right decision. The only decision.

'I did, but you're a beautiful girl, Lorelei. I let that distract me.' He paused to let it sink in. 'But, like I said, it's a busy time.'

'I distracted you?' Her tone had cooled to match his. 'Do you ask women to dinner who *don't* distract you, Nash?'

He released some of the tension in his chest. 'Okay, I'll lay it out for you.' He made his voice harder, grittier. 'The reality is you've got a media profile, Lori, and that's not going to work for me.'

There was a flat, astonished silence.

'Let me see if I understand this,' she said slowly. 'You no longer want to take me to dinner because you've read something about me in the newspaper?'

'No,' he said flatly. 'I don't want to take you to dinner because I don't want to read about *me* in the newspaper.'

He knew she'd taken his meaning because there was a pregnant pause.

'I'm sure that gets old for you quite fast,' she said, in a stiff little voice he didn't quite recognise as hers.

She paused but only to catch her breath.

'Is this about my father?'

He heard a note of that desperation she'd displayed on the street with her car, felt the give of his tightly leashed control and the threatened spill of emotions and desires he refused to give in to. Something about the way she kept going, revealing herself so openly, reminding him how unable to protect herself she had seemed this afternoon,

made this intensely personal—and it was working against his usual detachment.

He focused on pulling it back. He was good at
this. Reining it in. Being single-minded. He reminded himself it had been a long day, and this
woman had contributed to some of that length
with her theatrics.

'No, sweetheart, it's about you and your lack
of visible support and me being flesh and blood.
I made a mistake.'

He put finality in those four words. The conversation needed to end.

There was a sudden flash of silence.

His words echoed back at him, the harshness
of the message he was giving her making him
flinch even as he knew he'd given women the
brush-off before. Blunt always worked, and the
only casualty of this would probably be her ego.

'*Mais, oui,* you're a busy man.'

This time the heat in her voice was unmistakable and he relaxed a fraction. Angry was good.
He could put an angry, indignant woman behind
him.

'How inconvenient of me to distract you from
what's important,' she bit out. 'Here was I, think-

ing you were a gentleman, but you're just a *man,* aren't you? Like all the rest.'

He heard the catch in her voice.

'And not a very nice one.'

The phone went dead.

He dumped the cell, frustrated. For a moment he felt her in his arms again, the warmth of her, the delicacy, saw the way her tilted eyes grew round when she was uncertain. It was that uncertainty he'd heard threaded through her voice just now, and for a moment he knew he'd hurt more than her ego. For a moment he considered the alternative that she might have been genuine. That the witty, surprisingly refreshing woman he'd talked to in her kitchen this afternoon was the genuine article.

Then he dismissed it.

She was right. He wasn't a very nice man and that had brought him a long way.

What remained was the fact he'd blown off two meetings to spend time with a woman he didn't know, and it was time to play catch up. He hadn't got anywhere without being single-minded. He needed to get his focus back where it belonged.

He dressed, made the calls necessary to bring the people who could make things happen together.

Santo's Bar. Half an hour.

It was a quick drive from his apartment to the waterside bar. Nash, however, found himself taking the scenic route, driving down the glittery Monaco boulevards, remembering the first time he'd raced here. The narrow grid, the excitement of the danger inherent in this course above all other road circuits… He'd won and his life had never been the same again.

It had been an extraordinary ride—that race and all the races that had come before and after it, building up his motor-design business, Blue, the journey to this town, to this moment. It had happened against the odds, given his beginnings. He'd come from a background of squanderers. Money, talent, opportunity—all squandered on drink and women and bad bets. And that was just his old man.

Success had come quickly to him. Probably too quickly. He'd had a raft-load of hangers-on at the beginning of his career whom he'd bailed out financially. His father, his brother, old friends… They'd all viewed him as a lucky bastard, but he knew different. He'd worked bloody hard to get where he was, and he had learned to hold on to what he'd earned. He damn well didn't need another person who wanted something from him...

And just like that he was thinking about Jack. His brother.

He wasn't risking it again.

His expression hardened and he told himself if his gut was tied in knots it was only because Lorelei St James was clearly a premium lay and he wouldn't be having any. Animal attraction. It was why even now he swore the scent of her was still in the car, making him restless, angry, and making it hard to remember why he was denying himself.

Had she simply imagined it?

Had he really blown her off?

How had he phrased it? She had a *media profile.*

It was the trial. It could only be the trial.

Lorelei sank down onto the chaise in her bedroom and thought hard. What else could he have discovered? It wouldn't be difficult. She knew she had a social profile. She never Googled herself but she was aware that, like her friends, her name came up on different gossip websites.

She'd dated some known names in the past, but not seriously. She'd never been serious...or only once, when she was still a young girl and had thought a man telling you he loved you was reason enough to start planning a future—until you discovered he loved what he imagined was your trust fund. She'd never had one. Just a well-to-do *grandmaman* who'd kept her on a short leash and a small inheritance now gone.

Grandy had left most of her fortune to her charities. Lorelei knew she wouldn't have been human if she didn't sometimes think wistfully of how useful even a fraction of that money would be now, but she understood that Antoinette was punishing Raymond and not her. She had known one day Lorelei would be bailing him out.

Inevitably that day had come to pass. Unfortunately it had put the one thing Grandy had left her at risk: the villa.

But she wasn't thinking about that now. She needed to think about filling her evening, seeing as Nash Blue had changed his mind...

Possibly because he'd found a better option. A woman who was happy to go to Paris with him.

Lorelei's eyes narrowed. She snatched up her phone and began scrolling through the address book. Two could play at that game. She had simply masses of people she could call up…men who would break their necks tearing up the hill to take her to dinner. Her thumb hovered over names. Her heart fluttered hard in her throat. Why couldn't she just call?

Because… Because…

Fifi jumped up onto her lap, trying to climb her chest.

'Because I didn't want to be with anyone but him tonight,' she said, burying her face in her baby's warm fur. 'Dammit, Fifi, I was looking forward to tonight. I was… Oh, I'm being ridiculous. I'll make a call.'

She pressed Damiano Massena's number and he answered almost immediately. Clearly *he* didn't have a problem with her being a so-called distraction! But then, they had known each other for years on the party circuit. He was in town. He knew of an opening. It was always fun to go to an opening, and she knew he wouldn't press for anything more than her company. They'd sorted out that little crease in their friendship years ago. He was a womaniser and she was strictly hearts and flowers—not his type. He'd pick her up in an hour.

'Make it half an hour,' she insisted, pulling down the zipper on her dress. The last thing she wanted to do was sit around on her own.

She ended the call and let the dusky pink romantic confection she had chosen so carefully to wear tonight drop to her feet. She stepped out of it, leaving it puddled on the floor as she headed to the wardrobe. She'd put on something short and funky and guaranteed to get her all the male attention she could handle.

She tugged down a little gold party dress from its hanger. She'd go out, gossip, dance, amuse herself. Forget this had ever happened.

But she'd hold on to the fact he'd spoken so flatly, unemotionally, allowing nothing to alleviate his message: *I've changed my mind. You've got nothing I want.*

Turning around, she caught her reflection in the mirror—a tall, slender girl in an ivory slip and a simple string of pearls, who had dressed tonight with a particular man in mind. Her make-up understated, her hair smoothed carefully back into a deceptively simple knot.

The woman she actually was.

Unexpectedly a surge of sadness welled up from some place deep inside her. Was she never going to be allowed to be herself?

Lorelei inhaled sharply, ruthlessly dragging it all back in.

Irritated with her thoughts, and herself, she peeled off the slip and began the process of dressing as the woman she needed to be.

Santo's Bar was noisy, but it had shadowy corners where a couple of famous faces and the two founders of one of motor racing's more famous constructors could blend into the dark maroon leather and oak décor.

Nash sat on a light beer. He'd been off the hard stuff for almost four years. He didn't miss it, but every now and then a glass of single malt would have hit the spot. This was one of those nights.

He should be enjoying the company. It was all-male, and if they were a little loud and raucous, so was the bar. Antonio Abruzzi, Eagle's current star driver, was telling a story that had veered from off-colour to frankly pornographic. Nash had half an ear to it, but his attention kept wandering. He noticed a woman across from their table, winding a lock of dark hair idly around her finger as she talked, and instantly he was inhaling honey again, and flowers, and seeing the sun glinting off the sapphire-blue Sunbeam as Lorelei St James leaned back against it and smiled up at him with all the confidence of a very beautiful woman to whom a man had never said no.

Why in the hell *had* he said no?

He picked up his light beer and smiled grimly. He knew why. He was a goddamned expert on giving up what he liked for the sake of the bottom line.

It was just he was having trouble remembering what the particular bottom line was in this scenario. He'd swapped an evening with a blonde goddess for Abruzzi's stories and the watchful appraisal of the Eagle team who had signed him.

He stood up.

'Nash, man, where are you going?'

'Previous appointment.'

He shook hands with the Eagle guys, embraced Abruzzi and shouldered his way out of there.

He was going out as she was coming in.

Impossibly tall in vertiginous heels, she dwarfed the guy she was with—a thickset, strong-profiled Italian Nash recognised as the financier Damiano

Massena. They'd crossed paths several times in both business and leisure.

Massena was dressed in a long black coat, suitable for the cooler evenings, and Lorelei was a living flame in a gold dress. In the overhead neon lights it was difficult to tell where the fabric ended and her long, lithe limbs took over. She looked every inch the trophy, and Nash found he'd ground to a halt. His gut clenched. Because Massena had her and he didn't, he reasoned brutally.

She brushed past him, didn't look up, but he saw she had made dark pools of her eyes and a glossy invitation of her mouth. She looked like sin. She looked like every good reason he didn't want to get involved with her.

And most of the reasons he did.

But he was noticing other things, too. The evening was cool and there was a visible quiver to her bare limbs.

Why in the hell hadn't Massena given her his coat?

He inclined his head slightly and her gaze moved fleetingly against his. Massena said something to her, gave Nash an amused, man-to-man look, and ushered her forward.

The aggression rushed up from nowhere and he brought his hand down on Massena's shoulder. The older man turned around in surprise, his expression hardening as he read Nash's expression.

What in the hell was he doing?

He jerked his head towards Lorelei, paused in the door with her bare arms wrapped around herself, avoiding his gaze.

'Get her inside,' he said uncomfortably. 'She's bloody well freezing.'

He kept walking. Yeah, being single-minded had brought him a long way.

Lorelei was aware she was talking a little too animatedly in the car, as if the flow of words would stem the rising tide of feeling behind it. Since running into Nash she'd been preoccupied and not much company. Damiano was bringing her home early.

'Are you seeing him?'

Lorelei didn't even bother to demur.

'We only met today,' she admitted in a low voice. 'We had arranged to go out to dinner. He cancelled and I—'

'You phoned me. I'm flattered,' he drawled.

Lorelei put her hand on his arm. 'I phoned you

because you're one of my friends and I knew you would be good company.'

'Will you be seeing him again?'

'He's not interested.'

'For a man who isn't interested, *cara,* he has the eyes of a jealous husband.'

Lorelei swallowed, but couldn't ignore the flutter of excitement that observation engendered in her.

'A word of advice, Lorelei, from an old friend.' He gave her a wry look. 'Nash Blue is not a man for you to play with. He has been ruthless in the past with women a lot tougher than you, *cara.*'

'Ruthless?' Lorelei couldn't help the shiver that ran through her, although the limousine was climate-controlled.

'More so than me.' Damiano gave her a smile that reminded her where his own reputation with women had come from. 'And somewhat more effective with you, I am thinking.'

Lorelei didn't know what to say. She sat back and looked unseeingly through the dark window. She knew exactly how she felt about any man who was ruthless with women. She'd grown up with one. But she couldn't put aside all the sweet things Nash had done for her today. She was almost hugging them to herself.

In all the years since men had started following her with their eyes and making all sorts of empty promises no man had ever gone to so much trouble for her.

She could almost forgive him the cancelled date and the reasons he had given her.

Almost.

She had to ask. 'He's a womaniser, then?'

Damiano shrugged. '*Niente*—no more than any other rich and famous man, *cara*. I do know he's a man renowned for his self-control. He doesn't drink or smoke or brawl as far as I know. You say you met him just today?'

'*Oui.*'

Damiano threw back his head and laughed.

'I can't see what's so funny.'

'*Si,* I know, and that is what makes it even more amusing.'

Lorelei shook her head. She would never understand men. She relaxed a little, but as her turn-off grew closer she could feel the darkness edging in and a great unwillingness for the evening to end, for all the noise and activity to stop, to be alone. To think.

Yet when Damiano turned to her, all smooth Italian charm, and asked, 'Shall I see you inside?'

she shook her head without giving it a second thought.

'I'm a big girl and I know where the lights are.'

But as she entered alone the cold, empty weight of the house bore down on her.

She made her way upstairs, trying not to think about her debts and those warning letters and threats and what it would all inevitably mean… and somehow what flashed to mind was, *What if Nash Blue followed her home?* And if he did—if he drew up in her courtyard in that smart car of his, if his heavy tread disturbed the gravel, if he stood there in the dark and called her name like a sober Marlon Brando—what would she do?

What would she do?

'Tip a bucket of water on him. That's what I'd do,' she told Fifi as she flooded her bedroom with light. It was the only fully furnished room in the place, an Art Deco boudoir worthy of the silent-film star who had built this Spanish villa back in 1919.

Fifi stirred from her place of residence on the bed and trotted underfoot as Lorelei washed her face and undressed and cursed a bit.

'He thinks I'm media happy and looking for a

deep pocket,' she muttered. 'Well, we're neither of those things, Fifi.'

She went over to her escritoire and unlocked the deep drawer. Inside were months' worth of unanswered, unlooked-at correspondence from her solicitor and various legal firms who had handled Raymond's case.

As she settled herself down, pulling on her reading glasses and taking up a pen, she felt something akin to relief that she had finally started—until she began to read…

It was only when she was lying awake in the dark hours later, resting her chin on top of Fifi's warm little head, that she realised it had taken someone like Nash to come along today and force her to see her behaviour through his eyes, this house through his eyes and for her to find the courage to face her problems.

She supposed she could thank him for that.

She shivered and drew the coverlet up a little closer to her chin. It was a cold night, and that was another problem with this house—it was drafty.

Get her inside. She's bloody well freezing.

Had he really said that, or was it wishful thinking?

* * *

The next morning she was walking barefoot along the back terrace when her Sunbeam rolled up.

She put down her freshly brewed coffee and hurried out to speak to the two men who had delivered it. The car had been given a certificate of good health, she read, noting a few key parts had been replaced and the car had been tuned.

There was no bill.

'I don't understand,' she said uneasily.

'Compliments of Nash Blue,' said the guy with a shrug. 'She's a beauty, madame, take good care of her.'

Lorelei's fingers crumpled the report in her hands slightly before she realised what she was doing. *Compliments of Nash Blue?* She wasn't a charity case. She didn't need to be rescued.

Five minutes later a van was drawing up on the gravel drive. Lorelei looked up from the mechanic's report, recognised the insignia on the side. A boy leapt out and came towards her, bearing a large bouquet of red roses.

She took them in both arms, burying her nose in the rich scent.

Damiano. How sweet of him—and unnecessary.

She plucked out the card and suddenly the blooms in her arms took on a whole different meaning.

Forgive me. Nash.

CHAPTER EIGHT

LORELEI parked and jumped out of the roadster.

The car was performing like a dream.

Which made staying angry with the man who'd fixed it and sent you flowers all in one morning extremely difficult.

This entire situation was difficult.

She wasn't sure what she was doing here, but she figured something would occur to her when they came face-to-face. She had a half-formed notion that she would pull out her chequebook and insist he take payment for the car. But Nash, being one of those masters of the universe, probably thought it was his responsibility to make sure all the women in his vicinity didn't have to lift a little finger to help themselves.

Which just made her eyes roll when she saw his name in big letters on the marquee. Who named their company after themselves anyway? It just proved the enormous size of his…ego.

She made her way through the crowd queuing

on the perimeter of the fence. She gave her name at the gate and was handed her pass.

She'd dressed down in canvas top sneakers, skinny white jeans and a flirty gold lamé top that bared her arms and the backs of her shoulders. She'd pulled her hair back with a knotted blue scarf. But perhaps she was not dressed down enough.

People roamed about in windbreakers and casual gear, and as she made her way across the concourse she could feel eyes on her—as if she were some exotic animal released from the zoo come wandering among them.

She didn't know any of the volunteers, either. This wasn't her branch of the organisation. She'd actually had to ring the foundation that morning to organise a pass.

Her work for The Aviary was strictly high-end, and consisted of schmoozing for the big bucks at parties and receptions throughout the year. It was how she had met Damiano Massena and cemented her reputation as being impossible to refuse.

Every year she attended The Aviary Foundation's annual ball with him and set the tongues wagging all over again. But there had never been anything between her and the men she fleeced on behalf of the charity. She didn't mix business and pleasure.

No, there was no reason for her to be here—yet here she was, making her way through the crowd at a motor-racing track, soaking in the carnival atmosphere…honing in on the cars, the cluster of media, the excited children and their parents…

It wasn't hard to pick out Nash when he emerged through one of the gates from the track offices. It wasn't just his height but the way he moved— heavy, purposeful and a little intimidating.

There was a flutter of female speculation and Lorelei saw women literally pushing their way up to the barrier next to the track to get a better look. Fortunately big macho sportsmen had never done much for her.

Nevertheless, she fumbled in her handbag and touched up her lipstick with her compact, removed her scarf, knotted it around her neck and shook out her hair. A woman needed all her weapons about her, entering *this* arena.

Weaving her way through the crowd, she caught glimpses of Nash with the kids. He wore a black overall with white and green stripes and lettering and carried a bunch of helmets which he was handing out. The parents looked as star-struck as their offspring. The crew were crawling all over the cars in preparation, and there was a faintly vivifying smell of petrol fumes in the air.

She vaguely recognised another racing driver, Antonio Abruzzi, but only because she'd scanned the charity's internet site on the subject of today this morning, to avoid walking in blind. The lanky Italian was saying something to the media crew set up trackside.

Lorelei found she was quite close to the barrier and a little space had opened up. She slipped in and looked out across the track.

Nash had his back to her and was hunkering down to fit a helmet over the head of a young girl of about ten or so, with long dark hair. She had that po-faced look on her face Lorelei recognised from her young students when they were about to mount up for the first time.

He said something to her and she smiled, let him settle the helmet over her small dark head, and even from this distance Lorelei could see the care with which he buckled up the strap under her chin.

Something fluttered strangely in her chest, and

she found herself unconsciously touching the back of her neck where he'd stroked it yesterday.

He straightened and put his hand lightly behind the child's shoulders, ushering her towards the crew who were going to strap her in. Almost casually Nash glanced over his shoulder and their eyes met, locked.

Time seemed to slow down. The noise and jostling died away and Lorelei faced the undeniable truth that wild horses couldn't have stopped her coming down here today. As she ate him up with her eyes he turned around, those wide shoulders thrown into relief by his arms hanging at his sides—a typical masculine pose.

Vaguely Lorelei was aware of cameras going off around her as people lifted their phones to frame what anyone with an eye could see was a great shot. A male athlete at the top of his game, with the racing car just over to the right and Nash filling the foreground with his presence. Bigger, stronger, more impressive than just about any other athlete on the world stage.

His eyes were on her.

Lorelei lifted her chin. Now she knew what Simone was talking about.

He was a legend.

She'd just been distracted by the man.

* * *

Nash saw the defiance in her fine-boned chin as it poked in the air and thought, *No, you don't, mate. That little number is off the menu.*

She wasn't supposed to be here. After the incident with Massena last night he'd figured he had her pretty much read. She was a beautiful, privileged woman used to being pursued by wealthy men. Cullinan's tacky information had got her wrong. He'd been looking at the bottom of the survival chain when it came to women living by their wits. Lorelei St James was very definitely at the top.

He would have expected her to have moved on. Yet here she was, poised like a lily of the field behind the safety barrier, amidst a crowd of onlookers, looking as if she'd stepped out of *Vogue.*

In jeans.

But very expensive couture jeans, wrapped around a pair of impossibly long slender legs, lithe hips and a perfect peach of a derrière. She had a jaunty short blue scarf tied around her neck.

Despite the American accent he could hear underlying her voice she was every inch the Frenchwoman this afternoon. She'd dressed for a day at the marina, not a racetrack. This was probably as far inland as she'd ever been.

A golden girl in every sense of the word.

And she was gazing at him as if she expected him to stroll on over, swing her up into his arms and carry her off like the prize she was.

He couldn't say it hadn't crossed his mind.

She was so long and lovely, taller than most of the women standing around her, and possessing a fine-boned elegance that drew a man. Made him want to protect her, shelter her…do a great deal for her.

But he'd been down that road with this girl.

He'd spent yesterday mopping up her messes. Last night contributing to one of his own.

No more. Even if he had to take fifty cold showers, no more.

Let Massena or whoever take care of her.

He had some kids to run around the track, some photos to pose for and then he was taking off up the highway to his house in the Cap d'Ail for some well-deserved R'n'R before he flew out to Mauritius for meetings, then lockdown for training.

He was about to turn away when she raised her hand. It was just a little gesture, a half wave arrested by uncertainty, and it was the uncertainty that stilled him. His body suddenly felt tight, the blood in his veins heavy, his muscles tensing one by one in anticipation.

He was vaguely conscious that the crowd had surged forward as he headed over. This was an insanely public gesture to make. He conned himself it was a small event. Everyone was here by invitation. He doubted him chatting up a random blonde at a practice track was even going to make the internet despite all the phones madly going off.

Her expression had frozen. She looked like a mountain deer caught in a spotlight. She looked as if she didn't know what to expect. Something twisted in his chest.

He hadn't planned what he was going to say to her. He looked her right in the eye and she gazed unblinkingly back. And then he knew.

His tone was soft, low, deep. 'I'll talk to you later.'

Those amber eyes widened fractionally and she gave a slight nod.

He winked at the pair of gawping teenage girls standing next to her and strode off.

* * *

Most of the crowd had dispersed. Only the volunteers were cleaning up, the track crew coming and going. Nobody had questioned her wandering onto the track, walking alongside the cars, peering in.

It was getting late. Another half hour and it would be dusk. She glanced back towards the buildings. It was growing cooler and she only had her light cotton jacket. Maybe he'd forgotten what he'd said. Or maybe he'd been caught up. Or maybe he'd never intended to come in the first place.

She had put herself in this precarious position. She didn't chase after men. They chased *her*. Growing up watching Raymond work the female sex like a one-armed bandit had taught her that powerful lesson. To be the object of desire, not the one caught by desire. Therein lay hurt, abandonment and shame.

She knew she should go and get in her car and drive home. This had been a bad idea… Her idea of waving her chequebook at him and forcing him to accept payment for the Sunbeam seemed impossibly naive.

'Fancy a ride?'

His deep voice wrapped around her, every bit as delicious as the first time she'd heard it.

She turned around and found him a few feet away, dressed in jeans and a black T-shirt—so similar to the first time she'd seen him. All that thick dark hair was rumpled and a faint five o'clock shadow etched his strong jaw. His intense blue eyes gleamed in the fading light, watchful as a stealthy animal of prey. He was holding the straps of two helmets in one hand.

'Careful, Nash, what if someone sees us together?'

'Sweetheart, about fifty cell-phone cameras went off at once around us this afternoon. I think caution at this point is overrated.'

That wasn't the answer she wanted. She wanted him to say he didn't care and put her in his car anyhow.

'Come on,' he said abruptly.

He had opened a door. She stepped back. 'This one?' She looked doubtfully at the low-slung car.

'Blue 16. It won't bite.' His eyes were on hers, and why the expression in them reminded her of the wolf's paw reaching for Red Riding Hood she couldn't have said.

'Much,' she added dryly, reaching out a hand for the helmet.

He grinned.

Oui, the wolf.

He laid his helmet on the top of the car and moved in with hers.

Lorelei reached up to free her hair from the scarf but he was tangling his hand in it, tugging it away. Memory of the other time he'd touched her like this made her unbearably conscious of his big hard body only a hand-span from her own.

He must have felt it, too. 'Your hair,' he said, leaning in to inhale.

She felt his lips momentarily against the warm top of her head.

'Silky, soft… It smells like you.'

Breathless, Lorelei barely had time to react before the helmet was coming down, obscuring her pink cheeks, her questioning eyes.

He buckled the strap under her chin and Lorelei realised she'd been waiting for this ever since she saw him helping the little girl.

She'd wanted him to help *her* with the same attention to detail, deliberateness, care…

She felt like an alien in the helmet. It made her smile.

Nash held the door. 'Get in.'

* * *

Possession was nine tenths of the law, Nash figured. Once he had her in Blue 16 she was pretty much his. A court of law might argue the toss, but he wasn't much interested in anyone else's opinion other than the girl sliding into the high-performance car.

He hadn't planned any of this, but when he'd seen her standing over here by the cars, just waiting for him, everything male and predatory in him had fired up. If he was going to do this, he might as well do it right.

He couldn't help tracking her legs in those leave-nothing-to-the-imagination jeans, the curve of her peachy derrière as she slid into place, her small breasts pushing up against the disco-dolly top. Everything about her was lithe, delicate, incredibly sexy. Feminine. Everything about that, about *her,* got him going.

This was hardly the first time he'd used a touring car and high speed to get a woman in the mood, but it was over ten years since he'd felt it necessary and right now it felt new. It felt like the first time.

It felt incredibly right.

He swung in beside her.

He adjusted his own helmet and ran a sound-check.

'How do you feel about a bit of speed?' he asked through the mike.

'Exactly how fast are we going to be travelling?'

'Fast enough.'

She made an I'm-in-your-hands gesture.

How right she was.

He accelerated off down the track, keeping it simple, hugging the edges. Then he ramped it up. He loved this—those first moments when the car leapt from routine into supersonic and then there was just the rush.

The velocity shoved Lorelei back against the seat. She was grabbing the leather under her knees. He was going to scare the bejesus out of the little princess and then take full advantage of the results.

As the car flew down the track he could hear her panting breaths through the amplified mike. He could sense her tiny movements, her shakes and shudders. This was what he wanted. Her response, her subjection to his desires.

'Are you okay?' He spoke into the mike above the roar.

'Mon Dieu!' she panted.

And he knew, without taking his eyes off the track, that she was loving it. Every minute. And in that moment he wanted to give her the ride of her life.

She gave a shout as he rode the corner hard and tore down the strait. She squealed again, shoulders thrown back by the velocity, and he knew exactly what she was feeling because he'd felt it, too. The first time. Every time after.

This was why he raced.

It didn't explain why, with her, it felt new.

As he pulled back the speed and gradually rolled the car to a stop he could hear her breathing, her little murmurs of, 'Oh, my…oh, my…oh, my.' He knew he had her. What he didn't understand was why this felt so important.

They got out in silence.

He had his helmet off, but she was still unbuckling hers.

She threw her head forwards and back to release her flattened curls. They fell about her head in a messy tangle she didn't even try to smooth down as she lifted sparkling eyes to meet his. She was absolutely how he wanted her: messy, confident, excited.

Her lips parted and she was breathing hard and laughing. He knew exactly how she was feeling. The blood was surging through his body but it had nothing to do with speed or the adrenalin rush. She stepped towards him and he found himself making the same move.

Neither of them spoke.

All Nash could think was that he wanted her so badly he would have thrown her across the bonnet of Blue 16 if half a dozen other guys hadn't been within gawking distance.

Lorelei was looking up at him as if she shared every one of his thoughts.

'Wow,' she said softly. 'Thank you.'

'You're welcome,' he said just as softly.

Lorelei felt herself drift towards him and suddenly Nash was there, in her space, and the atmosphere between them was on fire.

'Come on,' was all he said, and she allowed him to take her hand. She knew what he meant.

He put her in his civilian car, drove the highway just on the limit.

Lorelei didn't ask him where he was taking her. She was too busy asking herself what she thought she was doing.

He'd barely touched her but her body was literally humming, and the tension in the car was doing her head in.

What was he thinking? Where was this going? Did it really matter?

He'd made it pretty clear he was in charge.

She watched the capable pull and push of his big hand on the gears, his long, strong arm, the cut of musculature running under the high sleeve of his T-shirt, the faint press of his chest as he breathed in and out, the way his jaw settled with precision as he concentrated on his driving. He was driving fast, but he was driving safely. He had made her feel safe since the moment she met him.

They were coming up to the turn-off.

'Your place or mine?'

It was the first time he'd spoken.

It was a question she couldn't hide behind, pretending this wasn't about sex. *I came to the track to find you, to let you know I was available to you…*

This never happened to her. Never. She was always cautious. She didn't meet a man and climb into his car and go home with him… Her breath hitched because she realised they'd come to a stop at the turn-off and she still hadn't answered him.

Nash cupped her chin, lowered his mouth to hers. Kissed her so sweetly she wanted to cling to this moment.

He did let her go. To decide for her.

'My place. It's closer.'

CHAPTER NINE

IT WAS the longest drive known to man, although practically Nash knew it was barely twenty-five minutes.

Lorelei's soft, sexy eyes on him driving were about as close to actually being skin to skin without taking their clothes off.

Her quiet bothered him, though.

Was she thinking about Massena? Did he need to go there, ask those questions?

He didn't share.

He was very, very possessive.

Okay, up until now that hadn't been the case with other women, but it appeared to be the case with *this* woman.

He'd been up all night thinking about her, visualising her with another man's hand on her waist, another man seeing her home. It was unreasonable. He'd blown her off. He'd been the one to call a halt. Everything he knew about her meant this was playing with fire.

The traffic in town was heavy. The light was leaving the sky and the boulevards were twinkling.

Nash shot the Veyron in and out of snags until they were mercifully prowling into the garage under his apartment complex.

Lorelei's chest was visibly rising and falling as they sank into the spotlit gloom, the darkness making the space between them more intimate and strangely tense. The excitement and adrenalin rush of the track had been infiltrated by reality. Nash remembered the things he'd said to her, virtually accusing her of being a media-whore, and yet here she was, despite all of that.

'About my car—' she said suddenly, her voice low and husky.

'All taken care of.'

'I know, but—'

'Why bother your head about those things?' He cut her off. 'It's nothing—a trifle.'

He could sense in her the need to say more, but all of a sudden she just subsided, looking down at her hands in her lap.

'The flowers were lovely,' she said instead.

Nash suspected she was trying to tell him something, but he didn't want to hear it. This wasn't about him fixing things for her in her no doubt chaotic life. Nor her eminently female desire to turn their liaison into something prettified with flowers and romantic gestures. He was here for one purpose and one purpose only: to work through this unholy desire to have this woman any way he could get her. All. Night. Long. They'd deal with the morning and where they went from there tomorrow.

For a guy who liked to plan, he was certainly enjoying making it up as he went along.

Which somehow was making this hotter.

'This is where you live?' Lorelei said a little breathlessly as they pulled up.

'Penthouse.'

She looked around. 'Must be nice being in the centre of everything.'

'It has its compensations.' Like now.

'At least you can park somewhere. So we're safe from the public ordinance.'

He liked her turn of phrase. He also liked that she was betraying a little feminine nervousness. *No, sweetheart, you're definitely not safe.*

'Nash?' She put her hand on his knee and for a moment he had the thought she was going to climb over and straddle him in the goddamn sports car. But then he realised that was his fantasy and she was just looking at him with a question in her eyes.

He didn't want to answer those questions. Except he was remembering something she'd said to him. *Here was I, thinking you were a gentleman, but you're just a man...like all the rest.*

He winged the door. 'Stay there. I'm coming to get you.'

'No, Nash—'

'Yes, Nash.' He gave her a slashing smile and in a fluid movement was out and around to her side of the car.

She looked up as he winged her door and hesitated a moment. He liked that hesitation. It made him want to reach in and scoop her out, to take instead of ask, but Lorelei seemed only to need a moment to make up her mind. She swung her lithe legs out, never taking her eyes from his, reminding him in every movement of her class and her poise and why he needed to be a gentleman… She literally stepped out of the car and into his arms.

He felt the delicacy of her bones, the softness of her bare arms as they wound themselves around his neck, the scent of blossoms and honey bees from her hair or her skin or simply the way she was. She brought her lips to his, confident and sure, before his mouth slanted over hers and his plans for tonight disintegrated.

He had intended to thrust deep, to make sure they both got the message that this was about dealing with a problem—sexual attraction—and overturn any idea this was a romantic scenario. They were both grown-ups. They'd both been here before. It wasn't going to go beyond that. Yeah, he was going to make her understand…

Until now, with her in his arms, one hand curled against his cheek, her lips soft and responsive beneath his, when the kiss turned tender and romantic and deeply fulfilling on some atavistic level he didn't want to explore. Not now.

Not when he had this.

He heard her sigh his name.

Obeying primal instinct, he tucked his hands under her bottom, shaping the incredible contours, and lifted her until she was sitting on the bonnet of the Veyron. Thinking he needed to get her sky-high and they were currently below ground, he wondered what in the hell he thought he was doing. But he needed to kiss her more.

One more taste, he promised himself, pulling

her in tight, feeling the warm skin of her waist as his hands delved under the silky fabric of her top. She wrapped her arms around his neck, her fingers tangling in his hair, making soft, satisfied little noises in the back of her throat that warned him this was quickly going to move out of control if he didn't get her off the car and somewhere private.

But it was Lorelei who broke the kiss, pulling back, eyes wide, breath coming fast, her whole body quivering. She looked around, not yet past caring.

Nash found himself bringing a hand to her cheek. 'There's just us. You and me.'

Her eyes softened. She touched his hand with her fingertips. It was a small gesture but he couldn't help entangling his fingers with hers, taking that small rough palm in his own.

'Inside?' she said a touch anxiously.

'Inside,' he agreed.

Nash lifted her from the bonnet and, taking her hand, strode to the elevator. He swiped the pass key and the doors closed. Even as Lorelei turned into his arms, pressing her face to the hard solidity of his chest, she felt the ground give way beneath her as they were hurled skywards.

She was breathing him in—heady, musky, spicy, hot male and, faintly, soap. The kind of plain soap she liked, not fancy. He was all kinds of good things, and even as her mind was running ahead, fantasising wild and wonderful, she wanted to cling to this moment, when it was just her, burrowing into the strength and solidity of him, and him tightening his hold on her.

She was vaguely conscious of a slight ping, the doors sliding open.

He lifted her as if she weighed nothing and carried her into his apartment.

As he kicked shut the door she took in the downlit expanse of modern masculine interior design. Smooth parquet floors, oyster walls and carpeting, and floor-to-ceiling windows that gave onto a multimillion-euro view of the velvety starscaped vista of Monaco's famous marina. Lorelei had been in some fancy homes in this town for parties and receptions, but she'd never made love in one. Faintly she thought there was something to be said for a sky-high room with a view when it came to romancing a woman.

There was also something to be said for being literally swept off her feet.

'Nash?' She brought her palm hesitantly to his cheek.

He caught her hand, kissed her palm fiercely and kept going. He kicked open a door and Lorelei could see two dressers, a huge eastern rug, a vast bed. A man's bed—so different from her own ice-blue silk Art Deco double. She registered chocolate-brown linens and a neatness and uniformity to everything that made her smile a little. But that smile faded as he released her, and she slowly slid down his body until she was standing on her own two feet before him.

She instantly felt a little dwarfed. His shoulders were impossibly wide, and the power of his sheer masculine dominance over her physically and, she suspected, sexually in this encounter gave her a moment of pause.

To even things up it would probably be best for her to step into his arms, initiate what she wanted, make her own demands… And yet as she waited to find her own rhythm in this dance all she felt was longing. For him to kiss her again, to be tender with her, for this to be somehow different from what she'd ever known before. She didn't know why this man, why...

'Let me see you,' was all he said, in a voice so soft it was velvet over her sensitised skin.

Obediently she toed off her canvas lace-ups, but Nash was already enclosing her in his arms, as if he couldn't help himself, his hands at the back of her neck, tugging at the ribbon that held her top in place.

'Let me,' was all he said.

So she let him. He was having trouble with it, and so close against him she could feel his tension. She could offer to help...

But when she lifted her hands he shook his head, bent his head, and his hot breath whispered against her ear. 'Let me.'

The ribbon gave and with infinite care Nash was peeling off her top, bending down as it fell away to press his mouth to the gentle swells of her breasts above the delicate floral pattern of lace just screening her nipples. He unfastened her fragile gold bra and it drifted to the floor, a cobweb of silk and lace. Lorelei registered the spike in heat between them as Nash viewed her bared breasts in the soft light, felt the splay of his large hands beneath the slight under curves, closed her eyes as his thumbs dragged across her nipples.

'You are so beautiful,' he told her.

She opened her eyes to find his expression first intent upon her own and then dropping down. She followed his gaze, drinking in the intensely intimate sight of his big tanned hands cupping the curves of her breasts.

'I want to see all of you,' he told her in a rough-ened voice.

Lorelei unzipped her jeans and his hands joined hers to slide them over her neat hips, to peel them down, helping her carefully to step out. His hands were slightly clumsy as they settled on her waist, and he was clearly drinking her in as she stood naked except for the tiny scrap of white silk that made up what passed for her panties.

'God, you are more than beautiful,' he said, almost reverently, and Lorelei, who had been praised for her looks by too many men, and had thought those words had long lost their ability to move her, let alone hold an ounce of truth, be-lieved him.

She stepped against him and began pushing his T-shirt up, baring an abdomen packed with muscle, a wide, hard chest lightly covered in dark hair. The feel of his skin under her hands was remarkably smooth and hot. His body was like a generator for heat. She ran her hands up over his deltoids as he lifted his arms to reef the cotton off, and she had her first proper look at what had been filling out those clothes.

He had a simply magnificent body—all height and large frame, which were the gifts of the gene gods. Although what he'd done with it, Lorelei thought a little light-headedly, the stripped, lean muscle and the grace with which he moved, wasn't to be overlooked.

No, she wasn't overlooking anything—including an erection she wanted to explore pressing against denim. But Nash didn't give her the opportunity to do anything about that as he dipped his head and began kissing her, lifting her so that her toes barely touched the carpet, his hands on her buttocks, moulding her against him. until she felt the long, thick ridge of that impressive erection pressed against her belly.

He released her slowly and dropped to his knees on the rug, his hands cupping her hips. She swayed in against him, shivering as he placed a hot kiss on her belly, and another, and another lower down. He was touching her there, through the silk, and then the silk was sliding down her legs and there was just his mouth, and Lorelei slammed her hands down on the back of his head, tangling her fingers through his silky thick dark brown hair, clutching as the muscles in her thighs convulsed. The faint ache in her hips that was always there after a long day on her feet was nullified by the almost painfully sensitive pitch he brought her to, until pleasure began streaking through her.

Her soft cries came unbidden as the dam burst and the waves of pleasure went on and on. Nash's tongue moved almost reticently as he gauged just how much she could take as her body convulsed. Just as she thought she was coming down he brought her up again, and again she peaked. When she was weak and clutching at his shoulders, swaying on her feet, he rose up like some kind of victorious sea god emerging from the deep. He gathered her in his arms and Lorelei, a little weakened and blurry from her orgasms, saw his eyes were wild, his tongue swiping a lower lip wet with her essence. He gave her a slow smile full of sexual promise and she just stared helplessly at him.

What had just happened? *Alors,* she knew what

had happened, but it had never happened to her before more than once at one time…and he had been so understanding of what she needed…

He lowered her onto smooth, cool sheets and her skin prickled not with cold but with anticipation as Nash stood over her. Slowly he began to unbutton his jeans with one hand, the other palming a square foil wrapper.

'Such a boy scout,' she approved a little unsteadily as the condom wrapper crackled.

'Always.' His eyes never once left hers and Lorelei watched as the denim parted, revealing his taut pelvic cradle, the cut marks of his abdominals, the deep grooves alongside his lean hips.

He shoved down his jeans and briefs in a single movement and gave her a slow smile as he saw the look on her face.

'I'm an engineer by trade, Lorelei,' he assured her with a wink. 'It's my job to make sure things fit.'

Lorelei watched him roll on the latex. She knew she ought to be taking the initiative, climbing into his arms and at least setting the pace, but somehow none of that happened.

Nash came over her, so big and dominant she

should have taken pause. He dwarfed her, yet her shiver had nothing to do with reluctance.

'Are you going to kiss me, Lorelei?' His deep voice teased her.

'Oui.' She put a hand to his chest, but instead of giving him a kiss she reached up instinctively and stroked his jaw with the backs of her fingers, wanting to stay the moment.

Nash stilled. The blue of his eyes darkened almost to black as he caught her hand and pressed a hard kiss to her knuckles, then he brought his mouth down on hers. A hot, passionate stamp of possession. He wanted her.

Everything Lorelei had decided, conjured, felt about Nash Blue did a somersault. Everything she'd been holding up to protect herself tumbled away. She had wanted him from the moment she saw him, which was a first for her, but she wanted something else and she wasn't sure what that was yet…

As his mouth roamed over her face, her throat, her shoulders, she inhaled the scent of spices and soap and man, splaying her fingers in his thick dark brown hair. She reached lower, spreading her hands over his broad back.

Feeling oddly vulnerable, she let her thoughts

flicker back to all the female interest in him today. She wondered what would have happened if she wasn't here. Was this what he did? Found the prettiest girl, scooped her up in his fast car and took her off somewhere…?

'Nash,' she said, perturbed by the anxiety she could hear in her own voice, 'what are we doing here?'

He smiled—a slow, unbelievably beautiful smile she had never seen before. There was an expectant tension in his hard muscled frame as he came over her, and instinctively she lifted her hand to his shoulder. His skin was so warm, his body so solid. She felt as if she could be anything, do anything, if she had this solidity behind her. It was a silly girlhood fantasy, long robbed from her by life and experience, but she was allowed it, wasn't she? Just for tonight? Tomorrow was soon enough to face cold reality, where she was on her own, but in the moment she had this.

She suddenly didn't care about all the other women, didn't care that she'd offered herself up to him at that racetrack. She didn't care about anything but the feeling of rightness having him here with her gave her.

'I believe we're making love,' he said, in that

deep, rich voice that flowed like warm honey through her limbs and made her pliant as she drew his face down to hers.

'Nash…' She said his name, pressing her lips to the base of his throat. 'Nash…' She said his name as she placed kisses along his jaw, nuzzled him. Wanted him.

She reached down and stroked his erect, heavy penis with her hand. His face so close to hers grew heavy with sensual pleasure, and his eyes beneath those sinfully thick black lashes were hot and sexual. He was so beautiful and so male Lorelei couldn't stop looking at him. She didn't want to stop. She felt powerful but also vulnerable at the same time, and never so female.

He took her hand and helped her guide the hard silken length of him to the entrance of the wet, hot heart of her body, his eyes never leaving hers. The head of his penis probed gently, and then he moved into her with one long, slow thrust.

Lorelei moaned, trying to accustom herself to the unfamiliar feeling of fullness.

'How is it?' His glittering blue eyes were close to her own as he brought their temples together.

'Wonderful,' she whispered, and in that instant she believed him about making love.

Filled by him, she wrapped her legs around him, taking him deeper. The passionate kissing, his mouth riding against hers as he surged inside her, the careful way he held her even as the pressure built for him—all coalesced into an intense emotional experience as she began the steady climb towards a blissful fall.

CHAPTER TEN

LORELEI lay in his arms, her face obscured by the cascade of her pale curls, her delicate beige-tipped breasts rising and falling rapidly as she slept. Faint tear-marks still glistened on her cheeks.

She had wept. She had pressed her face into the curve of his shoulder and wept after the first time they'd come together. Her whole body had quaked in his arms. He told himself sometimes that could happen for a woman, and he felt in Lorelei that her emotions were very close to the surface. But what didn't happen were the emotions *he* had felt…

Protective. Passionate. And stirred to action. Because those tears, he sensed, were not just a physical reaction to the intensity of what had happened in this bed.

So he had held her as she cried, and soothed her with his body, until somehow he was inside her again—and this time everything was so much slower, as if time itself had altered to fit the rhythm of their entwined bodies and he was giving her what she needed.

Sex he understood. Physical pleasure was one of the necessities of life—like water and sunlight and racing at high speeds around a track.

He wasn't entirely sure he understood this. What had happened in this bed.

It was nearing dawn. The first fingers of light had come creeping through the shadeless windows and there were pale shadows across the covers. The day was approaching and he didn't want it to come. He wanted to still time a little longer.

Watching her sleep, he felt almost as if he had captured some wild nymph from the woods and brought her to capitulation in his bed. She was so delicate, almost fey, he realised with a faint smile at the direction of his thoughts. She needed to be handled with care…and that should be sending warning bells off in his head, he thought, even as he stroked the silken curve of her bent arm.

His smile faded. Only hours ago he'd told himself this was merely the slaking of an appetite. He'd reasonably assumed his interest in her was powered by his sexual attraction to her body, as it had been with dozens of other women over the years.

But something else was at play here.

Even now he wanted to mark her so that other men would know she was his and wouldn't lay claim to her.

What am I doing here?

He didn't know.

Apart from the obvious, which was pressed against her hip and demanding his attention—or actually hers. It would be too easy to stroke her body to wakefulness and bury himself inside her, allow mindless pleasure to provide answers. But they had been doing that all night and his own stamina in itself had been a surprise. He'd never doubted his sexual prowess, but last night had been…rare.

Like the woman…

Nash touched the cluster of curls falling over one eye, hooking the silky weight behind her small ear, and she smiled sleepily, slowly opening her eyes. She lay there just looking at him and he was happy to let her look her fill. Her smile faded a little as she connected with his eyes, and she reached up and ran her index finger down the sweep of his jaw as if, like him, she was a little baffled by what had occurred.

'Is it morning yet?'

'Not yet.' His voice was rougher than usual, stripped back and raw. He needed coffee to lubricate it, but right now he wasn't thinking about breakfast.

Yeah, he could just about hammer nails with his erection but for a moment he wanted just to look at her.

Her hair lay about her head on the pillow like a bright halo. Her tip-tilted eyes were sleepy soft, her mouth swollen from his kisses. She appeared so delicate he would be a brute to initiate anything…

She sat up slowly, dislodging his heavy arm, which he obligingly lifted, a little surprised. But she was pushing back the covers, uncovering them both, still smiling, her eyes twinkling at him.

'Good,' she said.

Then slowly, silkily, she began to lead a trail of fiery little kisses down the centre of his chest, over his abdomen and lower, until he was gripping the sheet and forgetting everything but this.

* * *

Lorelei examined her reflection in the bathroom mirror. She'd done her best with the comb in her purse, warm water and a fresh toothbrush Nash had on hand in his cabinet. She hesitated as she held her lipstick up to her mouth, because the woman gazing back at her didn't need any make-up.

She had a glow.

Soft pink colour in her cheeks, a gleam in her eyes. Almost wonderingly she touched her lips. Her mouth looked frankly sensual.

She looked like a woman who had had a very good time indeed.

Smiling softly to herself, she dropped the lipstick back into her handbag and closed it, taking a longer look at the rest of her appearance. There was nothing worse than wearing clothes from the day before, but that couldn't be helped—and at least she wasn't in an evening gown.

Lorelei met her own gaze again, this time a little less confidently. This was a first for her, just to go off with a man and spend the night with him outside of a relationship. She knew he probably thought, given the chaos going on around her yesterday, that the walk of shame was hardly a first for her, but it was. She was careful in her romantic life to an almost fanatical degree. Men had to jump endless fences before they landed in her bed. She'd seen too much bed-hopping and sad, needy women growing up as Raymond St James's daughter to do anything else.

Ça va. She steadied her chin. She didn't have to worry. Even if she wasn't entirely sure what she was doing she didn't regret last night.

The tears, yes. She wished she hadn't cried. But that couldn't be helped.

She emerged to find Nash was talking into a cell phone on the balcony, the wind ruffling his hair. She was slightly taken aback by the sight of him in an Italian suit that lay close and faithful to the proportions of his fit body. He looked every inch the powerful and successful sportsman gone corporate, and here she was with damp hair, wearing yesterday's casual clothes. Talk about heading into the morning after with a disadvantage.

Sighing, Lorelei joined him, her desire to slide her arms under that expensive crease-free jacket, to encircle his hard, lean torso and enjoy the closeness of the moment held in check by the memory that, although last night had been intimate, she was old enough and wise enough in the ways of the world to realise they hadn't really done any talking of consequence. She didn't have a clue where she stood with him.

She wasn't entirely clear on where he stood with her, either. She'd gone into last night telling herself she had her eyes wide open, except this morning that pragmatism was curdled with a lot of fuzzy emotions she couldn't quite sort out.

So she settled for lifting onto her toes and pressing her lips to his freshly shaven jaw. Nash smiled, but he didn't make a move to end his conversation.

When he did it was to say, 'Ready? I'll run you home.'

Lorelei couldn't account for the cold trickle of disappointment that ran through her veins. It was perfectly reasonable that he'd be keen to get a move on this morning. It was after eight o'clock. He probably had a busy working day ahead—hence the phone call. She had to be at the equestrian centre at ten herself. They were adults. There were lives to get on with…

Dinner? *Oui,* dinner tonight, and then more… of this. *This* was making her tremble behind the knees and other places where she was tender. But also conversation. They would talk and clear the air and…

But perhaps this was it.

'Bien.' She injected a breeziness she suddenly wasn't feeling into her voice. It wasn't that diffi-cult—she did it all the time in social situations. 'Can I drive?'

He pocketed his cell, gave her a wink. 'No.'

It wasn't until they were driving out that she fully appreciated she had made a mistake. On their trip last night she had been the centre of his attention. If a meteor had hit the road he would have merely hung a left and driven on, intent only on their mutual destination.

This morning he looked what he was: a busy man with a schedule and not a lot of downtime. Preoccupied, a little tense, blocking her out. She was very clearly being driven home. This was it.

She told herself she was a grown-up. Neither of them had made any promises, and she wasn't really in any condition to be opening up her life to anyone at the moment…

They were on the corniche when he said, almost casually, 'I've got meetings today and tomorrow. In fact I'll be held up for the next few days.' He glanced over at her. 'How about I call you next week? We can spend some time together.'

Light exploded behind Lorelei's eyes. It was one thing to tell herself this was the way of the world. It was another to hear him speaking so lightly about the intimacy they had shared… *Spend some time together.*

For a moment she didn't know what to say. What was she supposed to say? *I thought I could handle one night, but I was wrong. Last night overwhelmed me. I'm feeling emotions I know have no place between us and now you're telling me you'll call me… It's not enough.*

Her mouth suddenly felt dry, her throat tight.

'I know it's not ideal after last night, but—'

No, not ideal. Nothing about this was ideal.

He looked over at her. 'I've got a lot going on, Lorelei. I didn't expect this.'

No, neither had she.

He sounded annoyed, but also faintly bemused. Memories of him kissing her so slowly and thoroughly, as if the pleasure of it was all he'd wanted in that moment, assailed her unmercifully. Unconsciously she found herself running the tip of her tongue along the rim of her bottom lip.

Nash shifted restlessly beside her.

Why had she thought she could do this and not be hurt?

'Or you could call me.'

His voice was almost gruff and she glanced over.

No, she couldn't call him. How could he possibly think she would call him?

'Will I?'

Nash looked at her sharply. 'What's the problem?'

'Rien.' Her voice sounded like a rusty gate. 'What could possibly be the problem?'

He had the temerity to glance at that big silver rock of a watch clinging to his left forearm. 'Okay,' he said slowly, like a man navigating a floor suddenly covered in glass shards, 'I will call you.'

'You do that.' She stared stonily out of the window, a thousand angry words jostling for some sort of order of merit on her tongue.

'What am I missing here?' he said, probably not unreasonably.

Bastard! What do you think? I'm just going to vanish out of your life?

She'd grown up hearing those sentiments.

Every woman her father had disappointed had flung something similar at him—as if he'd cared.

Douleur bonne, she might never have had a one-night stand before, but she certainly wasn't going to make a fool of herself by airing her messy female emotions now.

Non, she was a St James.

She lifted her chin. It had happened. Best to move on. She wasn't going to create a scene. From the tense silence emanating from Nash he was clearly expecting one.

The turn-off to her villa couldn't come quickly enough.

Nash barely had the Veyron at a standstill when she was fumbling for the door.

She swore, knowing that if she didn't get out of there fast she was going to embarrass herself. The door gave and she shot out.

'Lorelei.'

Nash's voice was peremptory—the voice she imagined he used on the track, with his pit crew, not a tone you used with a woman you had held in your arms and made love to.

Made love? It had been sex. What else could it be? They didn't know one another. She was a fool for expecting anything else…

She gave him his moment, not really expecting anything at this point, her hand still on the door.

'Do you want me to come in with you?' He actually sounded concerned—which was a joke.

She shook her head in disbelief. 'What's the point?'

Lorelei slammed the car door, and then wished she hadn't as she strode as fast as she could around to the front of the house. She rarely used the front entrance, but anger had blurred her thoughts. It had also blinded her, so she'd almost reached for the lion's paw front door handle before she saw the large padlock.

What on earth?

She gave it a tug. Was this some sort of joke? She seized hold of it with both hands and rattled. Then she banged even as she knew it was no use. She slammed her palms against the doors and then let them slide down and lowered her head, because it had finally happened.

Almost as an afterthought she noticed the large vellum envelope wedged under the door. She knelt down and picked it up, tore it open. She read slowly, the words like sticky toffee in her head. Was this even legal? The fact she didn't know was all the more damning. She should have known. She should have researched these possibilities. She should have been *aware*.

What had she been doing for the past months? *Rien*. Running around, blocking out reality, not making herself available to the people who could have helped her. Her solicitor, her accountant… her friends. And where had she been yesterday when this was happening? Pursuing a man. *Sleeping with a man who didn't care a jot for her.* She should have known!

Lorelei found she was trembling.

Non, she could deal with this on her own. She just needed to think logically.

Terese and Giorgio.

They would have some understanding as to what had happened here.

Fumbling in her bag, she dug out her phone.

The phone she'd been ignoring for days.

Sure enough there were several missed calls from the Verrucis and a message from Terese, she had rescued Fifi. Dialling, she got Terese's voicemail.

Fine—she'd ring for a taxi. Except she didn't do that. She dropped her cell into her bag and sank down onto the flags, her back pressed up against the door now bolted against her.

Strangely, she just felt like laughing. But she knew if she started it would end in tears, and crying wasn't going to change anything.

The worst had finally happened, and it was her own decision to delay and prevaricate that had brought her to this point. This was rock-bottom.

Until she heard the crunch of gravel, the tread of footsteps and slowly looked up.

Nash.

Mon Dieu, it just got worse. Could she just once have a personal disaster and not have this man witness it?

Yet something instinctive leapt in her body the moment she saw him.

'Lorelei?'

She clambered ungracefully to her feet, brushing herself down.

'What's going on here?'

'Rien.' She walked towards him, trying to divert him from the door.

Those blue eyes narrowed on her. 'Clearly. I don't respond well to games.'

'Fine,' she said, her voice high and airless. 'No more games. We had our fun. I need you to go.'

He was frowning down at her, and for a moment something about his anger penetrated the fog that seemed to have dropped around her. He was pounding out big, frustrated male and apparently *she* was the cause.

Gesturing at the drive, she repeated, 'Please go.'

'Why are you trembling?' He put his hand on her upper arm, his fingers closing firmly, as if he knew she would try to pull away.

'I'm not. I—' But it was too late. She was shivering so hard she thought she'd fall down. Wordlessly he pulled her into his arms and she was enveloped by all that strength and the lovely, familiar scent of him. *This is why,* she thought a little desperately, even as she struggled to be free. *This is why I'm a little crazy for him...*

'What in the hell?'

She knew he'd spotted the padlock.

He went still against her.

His voice was very low and resonant when he spoke. 'What's going on, Lorelei?'

When she refused to answer he released her and strode over to the doors, gave them a rattle.

'I've been locked out,' she said redundantly. 'The bank has foreclosed on my mortgage. I believe it happens if you don't meet your payments.'

Nash was silent. His hands rested on his lean

hips as he regarded her. Lorelei made herself meet his eyes. She wasn't going to be ashamed. She wasn't.

'A mortgage? You said you inherited this house from your grandmother.'

'I've had some debts,' she said, lifting her chin defensively. 'I had to raise the money somehow.'

She saw the moment he noticed the envelope beside her bag, and before she could move he had it open. Her stomach plummeted. He didn't say a word, just started scanning it. Lorelei turned away, facing out to the sea view she had come to know so well over the years.

'You haven't met your payments in over six months,' he said flatly.

'Non.'

There was a long pause. 'Do you have somewhere to go?'

Lorelei pulled herself together. *'Ah, oui*—of course.'

She turned around and her insides trembled.

Why did he make her feel like this? She hadn't wanted to get involved with anyone. Once you let another person in you were vulnerable, and she couldn't afford to let her defences down.

She looked into his eyes and saw his frustration and disbelief and she knew it was better to let him go.

Her chest began to hurt.

He picked up her handbag and strode towards her. He tossed it and she caught it reflexively.

'Get in the car.'

'*Pourquoi?* Why?'

He gave her an old-fashioned look and kept walking. Lorelei hesitated, but only for a moment, because she didn't know what else to do. He held the door for her, his expression grim.

'You don't have to do this,' she said stiffly.

'Consider it me being a gentleman,' he responded, looking faintly exasperated. 'Get in.'

She slid into the passenger seat, her fingers like pincers around her handbag. At the moment it was all she possessed. Nash still had hold of the envelope. He was standing at the front of the car, making a call on his cell. He looked tense. She couldn't blame him. This wasn't his problem.

Minutes later he jumped in beside her.

'If you could drop me in town—' she began.

'Yeah, I suppose I could.' He gave her a hard look, gunning the engine. 'Tell me, Lorelei, does all the drama ever get old for you?'

It was not the moment to lose her composure,

but the line between keeping it together and un-ravelling completely frayed a bit.

'I don't know, Nash,' she flashed back, want-ing to slap him. 'How about you? Do one-night stands ever get old for *you?*'

She knew it was unfair. She'd gone into last night with her eyes open. Except she was hurt-ing and her pride was currently being stomped all over.

He braked and shifted around. For a moment she wasn't sure what he was going to do and she backed up a little.

'Right...' he said slowly.

Right, what? Lorelei wanted to ask him what he thought he was doing when he threw the Vey-ron into First and she was flung back in her seat as he tore down the drive, sending stones and dust flying.

At the highway he swung right.

'This isn't the way into town.'

'No, this is the way to the airport.'

'Why are we going to the airport?'

'Sweetheart, those meetings I told you about aren't going to happen without me. I've got a flight to make, and as of...' he consulted his watch '…half an hour ago, the plane is fuelled and waiting.'

For a moment Lorelei actually thought he was saying he was going to dump her at the airport… until her brain caught up with her emotions.

'You're taking me with you?'

'Got it in one.'

'But I can't just leave. I've got to do something about *this*.' She shook the envelope, which had assumed gigantic proportions in her mind.

'It's pretty clear you haven't been doing anything about it for a long time,' he observed, giving a couple of the buttons on the console a flick. Music filled the cabin with a heavy bass line. 'A few more days isn't going to change a damn thing.'

Lorelei wanted to strike back at him—not just because he was imposing his wishes on her, but because he was right. She hadn't been looking after herself. The Scarlett O'Hara 'tomorrow is another day' shtick wasn't working for her any more, and this was the price she paid. Just as she hadn't thought through last night. She'd gone into his bed like a kamikaze pilot and wondered why she'd crashed and burned.

There was no way she was going to Paris with

him…she wasn't some little sex doll he could just carry around with him, picking her up and putting her down…

Her thoughts came staggering to a halt. Simone was in Paris. She could find shelter with her best friend, ride out this storm.

'Very well,' she said stiffly. 'I agree to come to Paris with you.'

He shot her an amused look. 'Paris? Who said anything about Paris?'

She was a little taken aback—by that glimpse of humour more than his words. Did he think this was *funny?*

'Where are you taking me? You said meetings. Blue has offices in Paris. I assumed…'

'Mauritius,' he said flatly, his expression firming.

Sun, white sand, turquoise-green sea. Bliss. Oh. *Oh…*

'But I don't have any luggage, my passport, clothes.' Even as she protested she was rummaging around in her bag. '*Ah, oui,* I do have my passport,' she said faintly. Was she really going to fly to Mauritius?

He gave her a look she recognised from last

night. 'You don't need luggage. You don't need clothes. You won't be getting out of bed.'

Lorelei narrowed her eyes. 'Is that so?'

Nash smiled wryly, his eyes back on the road.

'And just in case that isn't clear enough for you, Lorelei,' he drawled, 'last night wasn't a one-night stand.'

CHAPTER ELEVEN

LORELEI was stunned by the natural beauty of the island below as their seaplane coasted in over turquoise water. Mountains rose up against a pale sky and the forest beneath looked thick and mysterious.

She turned to Nash and asked, 'what are they growing down there?'

'Sugar-cane plantations. It's a big part of the economy—apart from tourism.'

'I take it you haven't come to harvest sugar?' she commented, a little smartly.

He hadn't told her much of anything over their long flight. He'd buried himself in work and she had watched in-flight films and tried to avoid thinking about the mess she'd left behind her at home.

Right now she noticed his expression cooling both in regard to her *and* the view. His arm around the back of her seat told her she was still a welcome addition on this trip, but his eyes were those of a man who didn't share private or working details of his life with anyone.

Apparently being in his bed for one night didn't give her the right to ask any questions.

Which also begged the question whether he expected a second, and whether she would grant it.

'My meetings have nothing to do with us,' he commented, as if that was all that needed to be said.

The resentment she had been trying to suppress since he'd high-handedly made a pretty big decision for her and run roughshod over her wishes reared up. What made it worse was the fact she knew she'd brought this all on herself by burying her head in the sand all these months. Except it wasn't only about that, was it? It was to do with intimacy, and having this knowledge of him now, and realising for him it wasn't the same.

Suddenly angry with herself for being so boringly *female* and needy, she jerked around. 'Damn you, Nash Blue. I don't need to be rescued—by you or anyone.'

Nash had removed his jacket when the heat had hit them on landing on the African coast, and he had looked more relaxed over the last half hour, with his shirtsleeves rolled up, than he had on the plane when he'd worked, taking calls, scrolling through documents, preoccupied.

Now he sat forward, tension in every line of his body.

'Is that what you think this is?'

'What else could it be?'

Her entire body was quivering.

'How about me ensuring this isn't a one-night stand…which I assumed was upsetting you. Something, I might add, that was never my intention to begin with.'

'*Bonne chance* with that, as I have no intention of sharing your bed.' She stuck her nose in the air. She knew she was being ridiculous as she did it, but everything about this situation was making her feel diminished.

He regarded her as if she was speaking nonsense. 'I'm beginning to suspect this is not about me, Lorelei, but you. Am I to take it those guys you've dated in the past haven't treated you all that well?'

Lorelei froze, feeling hunted and cornered.

'My affairs are not your business,' she said shortly. 'I do not ask you about other women… of whom I'm sure there have been far too many.'

'Possibly,' he responded, unruffled.

She snorted. She didn't want to think about his track record.

Hers was pretty tame, although he didn't have to know that. Her handful of boyfriends consisted of a visual artist, a poet, a writer and a classical musician…the last breaking up with her over two years ago, just as the perfect storm of Grandy's death and Raymond's arrest had broken over her. Truth told, she was rather grateful he had, as she couldn't possibly have supported him emotionally through the crisis. That was her role in all her relationships. She provided material support and emotional strength. She was, in effect, what she had always been with her father…the grown-up. And in the end every last one of them had foundered on the rocks because deep down what she craved…a man who could match her in strength of purpose…was the very thing she avoided like the plague.

She had seen enough unequal relationships paraded before her. It was a trap for a woman. She would always call the shots, hold the purse strings. She would keep herself independent— and strong.

Which was making all of this so very scary.

Because this man beside her, looking at her as

if she were a puzzle he was determined to solve, was everything she should be running from. Dominant, wealthy, definitely calling the shots, and right now he had hold of those purse strings. None of that would really matter, except he filled her thoughts and took over her body and made her feel in a way she never had before.

She was vulnerable to him.

She had been from the moment she'd set eyes on him.

Why else had she slid into his car last night and abandoned her inhibitions in his bed? She wasn't being free with her favours. She was being optimistic with her heart.

Not that he would understand. She doubted Nash had ever been vulnerable to anything.

'I have some rules,' she said, smoothing back her curls. 'I expect you to abide by them.'

'This should be good,' he drawled.

'Don't patronise me, Nash. I want separate rooms.'

He regarded her as if she'd sprouted wings.

'I just feel there's too much inequality at play here.'

Oui, Lorelei, that's putting it mildly.

She didn't want to be one of his shiny toys,

like the Veyron or the penthouse apartment in La Condamine. She had seen too much of it growing up…a price tag attached to love. It was why she kept her charity work for the Aviary Foundation separate from the rest of her life. She had never dated any of the men whose parties and functions she attended on a regular basis, and it hadn't been through lack of being pursued. She just didn't want to blur those lines between spruiking for the charity and spruiking herself. The idea terrified her.

'I'm not a toy for you to play with, Nash.'

Her whole body quivered as she spoke.

'In what way have I treated you like a toy?'

'I don't need luggage. I don't need clothes. I won't be getting out of bed,' she imitated sourly.

Nash's expression of pure male bafflement would have made her laugh in any other frame of mind. Right now she just wanted to hit him.

'It was a joke!'

She looked away, staring blindly through the plane porthole at the same view that only minutes ago had held her spellbound.

'Just don't call me doll any more,' she muttered.

'Sorry?'

She jerked her head around. 'I don't like being

called *doll*. A doll is something you put in a box when you finish playing with it, or put on a shelf like a trophy.'

Nash was silent. He was examining her face as if translating Sanskrit.

'Have you finished?'

'*Non*. I didn't in a million years imagine when I went to your apartment last night I'd be ending the next day with you in Mauritius.'

'As I hadn't told you I was flying out to Mauritius, I'm sure you didn't,' he observed dryly.

He was being deliberately obtuse.

'I'm not that sort of person.'

'*What* sort of person, dare I ask?'

'One who freeloads.'

Nash threw back his head and laughed, the sound rich and warm.

'I'm glad you find it so funny,' she said stiffly. 'I can assure you nothing about this situation amuses *me*.'

Fed up, Lorelei folded her arms and averted her face. Still in yesterday's clothes, she felt creased and wilted and distinctly at a disadvantage. Whilst he found it funny and had it all under control.

'Lorelei.' He spoke patiently, the amusement

still in his voice. 'I apologise for not telling you last night I was going away.'

She hated this—him being the cool, calm male and her being the hot, hysterical female. She'd been a witness to this scenario before and vowed she'd never play this role.

But who was forcing her into the role? Didn't she have a choice here? She was letting the inequalities of the situation play with her deepest insecurities and it wasn't serving her. The fact she was in this seaplane with him, coasting towards the runway, was proof enough that last night hadn't been all on her side.

'Apology accepted,' she said stiffly, wondering if they could start this all over again, with her being sexy and playing hard to get, instead of frustrated and sulky because she was in yesterday's clothes and he hadn't kissed her *once* since she'd slipped from his bed this morning.

'And I do not consider you a freeloader.'

She made a dismissive gesture with one hand, keeping her eyes averted.

'Is this about your father?' he said, cutting right through to the heart of the matter.

She raised her eyes to his. Grim.

'I don't talk about my father. Ever.'

He looked at her for a moment and then inclined his head. 'If that's what you wish.'

No, it wasn't. She wanted to wail and thump with her fists and bemoan Raymond and the fix he'd left her in, but none of that was Nash's concern and she wasn't laying more of her troubles at his feet. She'd dealt with this on her own thus far. She would continue to do so.

'Except you're not dealing with it, are you, Lorelei?' whispered a niggly little voice. *'You're winging over the coast of Africa with a man who delights and terrifies you in equal measure because he's seen what a mess you've got yourself into and he's trying to help.'*

All of a sudden she was beginning to feel ungrateful and childish.

She suspected a big part of her was trying to find something to take her attention off what she was trying resolutely *not* to think about—the mess she'd left behind her at home.

A mess that wasn't hers to begin with.

Those defence measures against the impossible weight of debt and the expectations she had laid upon herself to keep her family legacy intact were barely holding up any more and so she was lashing out. She also knew one of the reasons those defence mechanisms were no longer working had something to do with the man sitting beside her. He'd opened up vulnerabilities in her she was having trouble overcoming. Hence last night's tears.

She'd seen puzzlement and frustration in him several times as he'd come face-to-face with her issues back in the Principality, and it was getting harder to hide them from him.

She suspected it was one of the big reasons she hadn't had a relationship since Raymond's arrest. Why she had put distance between herself and her friends.

She should be putting distance between herself and Nash—especially when he was being so mysterious about exactly what they were doing here. The problem was, she couldn't separate mind and body. Her emotions were involved, as last night attested. If she slept with him again she was going to open more of herself up and there would be consequences.

'So these mysterious meetings—are they going to take up all of your time?' She tried to change the subject.

'Not entirely.' He smiled at her, as if he understood she was finding this difficult. 'I can, however, assure you you won't be bored, Lorelei.'

'Non?' she said snippily, knowing exactly what he was implying. 'I'm sure the island offers many attractions for tourists.'

Unexpectedly he tugged gently at the rogue curl she could never keep out of her eye, sliding it carefully behind her ear.

'Still fighting me, Lorelei?'

She looked away, out of the window at the land coming ever closer, and thought, no, she *wasn't* fighting him—and that was the problem.

'I can't get over how gorgeous it all is,' Lorelei confided as they drove the beachfront road in a Jeep. She'd teased him when he'd dumped their driver on the tarmac, telling him Freud had a few theories about his need to call the shots.

'Yeah, and I've got a few theories about Freud,' he'd responded, lifting her into the Jeep, enjoying her shriek and subsequent laughter. It was as if she'd decided all on her own to stop fighting him. It was impossible not to take in the scenery through her eyes as she chattered and pointed out landmarks that in the past he'd taken for granted.

Tall latania palms swayed along the roadside,

and tropical flowers flashed out of the under-growth as they sped past.

'You've brought me to paradise.'

Nash smiled to himself, finally comfortable with where this was going.

Lorelei had shied a little on the seaplane, and put on a bit of a performance, but he wouldn't have expected any less from the show pony she most definitely was. He realised he enjoyed that about her—the unpredictability. His life was usually so ordered. He didn't mind accommodating Lorelei's eccentricities. Outside in the late-day sunshine, with the fresh air whipping her curls into a frenzy, she seemed to have shrugged off her insecurities and was now embracing what he had to offer.

'Consider it part of the service,' he responded easily.

She flashed a smile at him and he was surprised at how good it made him feel.

He wanted her to be happy, he realised. He didn't like seeing that weight in her eyes as if the load she was carrying had been with her for too long. He suspected it was to do with that gaol bird father of hers. He could suggest to her cutting the cords that bind, as he'd done years ago with his own, but he doubted Lorelei would thank him for it.

He'd known since last night that she wasn't quite the hard-headed little mover and shaker those reports he'd initially paid attention to had painted her to be.

As they drove the leafy road circling the resort Nash watched some of the animation leave her. It wasn't his favourite place. A world-famous destination, sure enough, but they might as well not have left Monaco. The place dripped glamour and elitism, with groups of women in couture beachwear and jewellery, and men driving low-slung ego-extension cars.

'If you'd prefer we can stay here,' he commented as they cruised past the ostentatious entrance, 'but I've got a place on the beach. It's a lot more private.'

'Naturellement.' She gave him a small smile. 'I would much prefer that.'

Unable to credit how good he felt, Nash increased speed and they shot down the beach road, heading up and over a rise. He heard Lorelei catch her breath as they plunged into tropical rainforest.

'Oh, this is beautiful,' she gasped, and as if to

verify her words a brightly plumed bird swooped through the canopy of tree branches above them.

His bungalow was down on the shore—one of several private homes along this exclusive stretch of east coast beachfront. He had designed it himself with a local architect, the focus being on bringing the tropical forest right up to the doorstep and the ocean into the west-facing rooms.

Lorelei was quiet as she looked around, before turning to him and saying, 'This is most lovely, Nash. You're very lucky to have something so fine.'

'Not too modern for you, Lorelei?'

'Let me tell you I would kill to live in something so cutting-edge.'

'Then why the Spanish villa?'

Some of the animation slid away from her face. 'My *grandmaman* wanted me to have it.'

'You could always sell it.'

Lorelei turned away. He followed her through the dining area and out to the rear of the house, where windows gave way to the ocean, telling himself he didn't want to look any closer, dig any deeper.

He closed a hand around her lithe waist and she started, as if she'd already become unused to his touch. It made him more possessive. He found himself surrounding her, wanting to put himself front and centre in her life. He put it down to never accepting second place.

She removed his hands, walked away.

'Why don't you sell it?' he asked abruptly.

Lorelei shrugged her delicate shoulders.

Frustration rippled through him.

He thought about the fact that in a couple of hours he'd be sitting down to dinner with the Eagle reps, who also happened to be long-time mates.

His rather brutal earlier thoughts on the subject had been that she could entertain herself, and he'd get away as soon as he could.

But the guys would be bringing their wives. Her remark—*I'm not a toy for you to play with*—nudged him.

The problem was if he took Lorelei she'd be privy to his story before it broke in the press. He tried to picture her as a media leak but all he could see were her sleepy, sexy eyes when she'd climbed on top of him in the early hours of this morning and taken him almost shyly into her slippery hot body. Those little cries of completion as she'd reached her peak had made him feel like a god, and how sweetly she'd curled in his arms afterwards and fallen asleep, still holding on to him.

He groaned in frustration and ran a hand through his thick hair.

'We're meeting some friends of mine for dinner at eight,' he said gruffly. 'I had some clothes sent up for you. I guess you'll find them in the wardrobe.'

She turned and smiled at him. '*Merci beaucoup,* that's very good of you.'

He almost laughed. *This* she didn't fight him on.

Except she'd been fighting him ever since she'd climbed out of his bed.

He didn't understand her.

He didn't understand himself when he was around her. When he'd put her in Blue 16 on the track he'd only been thinking about a night, but this morning all he'd been thinking about was how soon they could be together again. He came up behind her at the glass doors leading onto the deck.

Today had been a long one for her. Even now he could see the faint mauve shadows under her eyes, a certainty fragility hovering over her. It was possibly the wisest course to leave her here. To go to dinner with the Eagle reps and give Lorelei some space. But it wasn't just about giving her space, he acknowledged. He cared about her feelings.

Frankly, he didn't want to make things any harder for her.

'Nash, the ocean is right on the doorstep!'

'It's a matter of perspective. There's a good twenty feet between the foundations and the surf, and this stretch of water is effectively a lagoon. It won't rise.'

'It's beautiful,' she said, looking up at him with an open face, and he smiled a little because she clearly cared nothing for the logistics and everything for the magic.

And wasn't that how she seemed to live her life?

He couldn't resist stroking her silken hair. Everything about her was touchable and soft and… yeah, he wanted to know her better.

But she wasn't an ingénue, and he wasn't a man looking for dependants. This was about her being a reward before he hit lockdown for training and him being her man of the moment. If he kept it that way this should work out for both of them.

If there was something beguiling about Lorelei's smile as she looked up at him it was to do with the tropical light and the promise of the night ahead. So he decided to follow her lead for once and just accept the magic.

'Yeah, it is beautiful,' he responded a little huskily, and framed her face with one hand. At last she opened up enough to let him kiss her. 'Second only to you.'

He tasted her—the softness of her lips, the sweetness of her breath—and the magic happened all over again. He knew he'd be taking her to dinner.

'So I'm to be your sex doll?'

Nash schooled his expression into something neutral as Lorelei emerged from the master bedroom, a tiny scrap of lace nothing dangling from her little finger.

He'd rung his housekeeper here at the bungalow and told her to organise some clothes through several boutiques at the resort, giving a vague approximation of size and stressing *sexy*. The helpful women at the boutiques had clearly interpreted this as less being more. He wasn't complaining.

Lorelei stood in the doorway looking unimpressed, although he did detect a tiny quiver about her mouth that told him she was trying not to laugh.

She looked sensational in an ankle-length orange pleated silk chiffon dress, embroidered with tiny crystals at its plunging neckline. It was the neckline that had his attention. His mouth was suddenly dry.

Belatedly he noticed she had swept her hair up into one of those sophisticated knots that took lesser women hours, and wore delicate crystal earrings. The juxtaposition between the ice goddess standing before him, her short sharp nose in the air and the little bit of erotica hooked over her finger finally dragged his eyes away from her braless breasts.

'You can be whatever you want to be,' he corrected, coming towards her. 'You could try being yourself.'

Lorelei's lips parted slightly.

'I am being myself.'

He plucked the bit of lace from her hand. 'Then there's no problem. I've seen your lingerie, Lorelei. You wear a great deal less than this.'

'Currently I'm not wearing any, but I would have preferred the choice.'

Nash's mind went blank.

'You look very smart,' she said with an arch lift of her brows.

Endeavouring to get himself under control, he rasped, 'It's the tailoring.'

A little smile sat at the corner of her mouth, as if she was very well aware of something else. 'Shall we go?'

The restaurant was open-air, on the beach, and the rhythm of local Sega music thrummed as a backdrop. Lorelei sipped her iced water, too nervous to risk a glass of champagne.

On the charity circuit she was always working to get people to like her, to respond to her, to open their chequebooks. Tonight she wasn't sure of the rules.

The large table was peopled with several couples: various identities from the motor-racing world, and one retired driver, Marco Delarosa, so famous even Lorelei recognised his face instantly.

This was Nash's world, both corporate and competitive, with the glamorous edge provided by sport. She wasn't quite sure what was going on, but amidst the thumping testosterone-fuelled talk about commercial deals and television rights she became conscious that Nash was talking about racing again.

This was confirmed when Nicolette Delarosa leaned over and murmured, girl to girl, 'We need to form our own team—at least then we might be a viable part of this conversation.'

A team.

One by one the pieces fell into place.

He was staging a comeback.

With Eagle.

This was why he was so media-shy. This was why he'd cancelled their date. Yet here she was, at this table, privy to the big secret.

She couldn't understand why, but Lorelei felt a frisson of unease.

Seeking reassurance, she flashed her gaze up to Nash beside her. His body language was relaxed—shoulders loose, open. He was fully himself because he was among friends. This was nothing like what she had built up in her mind. He wasn't treating her like a rich man's arm candy, as she had feared, those were her own insecurities.

It was clear in this company that when Nash was private it was because he needed to be—monosyllabic, as Simone called it, because everything he said publicly was weighed and measured. With his friends he was this relaxed and good-humoured man.

His thick black lashes were screening the full impact of his eyes, but although he was listening to Delarosa she knew his attention was on her. Had been on her all evening.

As if sensing the shift in her thoughts he lifted his lashes and there were his intense blue eyes. Lorelei found her pulse was fluttering wildly out of control. He was looking at her as if she was naked under him in bed.

Mon Dieu, other people would see…they would know…

The hum of conversation died away and there was only an incredible stillness. It seemed to happen between them again and again—his eyes and her heartbeat and that elemental force that shook her when she was in his arms. Only his arms. *Only him.*

What was going on? She couldn't fall so far and so fast for this man.

Almost to rip herself free from the spell he'd

cast, she reminded herself that Nash was a public figure because of his sport, and he was about to enter that arena again. Did she really want to be the woman on his arm? To face that sort of intrusion into her personal life?

'Lorelei St James,' said one of the women, her voice a little too loud. 'I *knew* that name was familiar.'

All of a sudden her musings ground to a halt. In that instant she felt Nash's hand close over hers under the table.

'Pardon?'

'It has to be over a decade ago now, but I remember seeing you at the World Equestrian Games.'

Lorelei released a hurried breath. *'Ah, oui*—many years ago.'

'I jump myself. My family breed Arabians.'

She felt Nash's hand turning hers over, his fingers finding those calluses on her palm. All of a sudden she felt horribly exposed, and she didn't quite know why, but to pull her hand away would be the first step to getting up and walking out, and she was done with that sort of reactive behaviour. It didn't serve her. So she mastered her nerves and continued to smile at the woman. To answer questions. To discuss the relative merits of each breed.

Couples were dancing to an old Cole Porter tune outside, and Nash suddenly pushed back his chair, interrupting the woman's flow. He got up, offered Lorelei his hand.

'What a brilliant idea,' said another of the women.

Lorelei followed him out, and the moment she was in his arms he caught one of her hands and turned it palm-side up. She didn't want to struggle to free herself so she let him.

He rubbed his thumb over the calluses.

'Why didn't you tell me about these?'

He didn't sound accusing, just genuinely surprised.

'You never asked.'

'You're right. I haven't asked. But I'm asking now.'

She tugged her hand away. He let her.

'They bother you? The calluses?'

'They're not very feminine,' she said tightly.

'I disagree.' He put his hands around her waist, drew her close. 'You've got capable hands.'

Lorelei leaned in against him. 'They used to be

my gift,' she said unthinkingly, seduced by the sudden proximity of his size and strength.

'Your gift?' he prompted

'I evented. Rode horses in dressage and show trials. I was quite good.'

'How good?'

'Good enough.' She felt slightly awkward. 'International standard.'

Nash stopped swaying her in his arms. He was looking down at her as if she'd said she once had two heads.

'I've surprised you,' she said, a little more crisply.

'You've impressed me,' he said slowly. 'But you said you rode, in the past tense. Why did you give it up?'

'I had an accident. It's made any sustained time in the saddle difficult.' She hated this part. It was the reason she never talked about it. People either felt sorry for her or dismissed it as a minor disappointment. Both rankled. Almost in sympathy she felt the echo of phantom pains in her hip flexors.

'How did it happen?'

His voice was low, and it was easy to forget they were on a dance floor. It was as if they were in their own private little world.

'I was twenty-two. I came down over a jump, and so did the horse. He landed on me.'

Nash stilled.

'I survived—obviously. It took several surgeries and a lot of physio, but I'm able to ride recreationally again.'

'How long were you in recovery?'

'Two years.'

She saw him absorb that information.

'Those marks on your hips?' he said a little roughly.

Her eyes darted to his. He'd noticed. They were so faint. Did he find them unattractive?

'We all have scars, don't we?' she said slowly. 'It's a part of life.'

Nash surprised her by sliding his hands subtly onto her hips. 'You hide yours very well,' he said.

'What about you?' she challenged. 'Where are your scars?'

He looked her in the eye. 'I wear them for the world to see,' he answered. 'Every time I race.'

Race, present tense.

She wanted to ask him about it but Nash bent down and said in her ear, 'And your old man? Is he really a gigolo?'

Lorelei pulled her arms free and went to walk away, but Nash had her tightly around the waist.

'Touchy, aren't we?'

She flashed active dislike at him and said tightly, 'He's the best on the Riviera.'

'There you go,' he said lightly. 'Not so hard talking about it, was it?'

'Have you finished?'

'I'm just wondering,' he said, continuing to sway her lightly, 'how many other secrets you're hiding.'

Lorelei looked away. 'Nothing that could possibly interest you.'

'On the contrary, Lorelei, I have a feeling it's all going to interest me. Come on—we'll get your wrap.'

'I don't understand. Where are we going?'

'Where do you think?'

CHAPTER TWELVE

FROGMARCHING her across the sand in heels only got him so far. Lorelei ground to a halt and swiped off her shoes, then threw them at him. He'd seen her aim before. He had the sense to sidestep and duck.

'You worked the crowd well tonight,' he called after her.

'I wasn't working,' she responded. 'I was just being myself—not that you would know anything about that.'

Nash caught up with her.

'Hard work, is it? Prising open those wallets?'

She stopped dead. 'Why are you making it sound underhand, as if I have other motives?'

'I'm sure when you were on Andrei Yurovsky's yacht last summer you had the best interests of the charity at heart,' he responded. 'And when you were in New York with Damiano Massena earlier this year it was purely a charitable impulse.'

Lorelei blinked rapidly. 'You're jealous,' she said as if this were a wonder.

'No, sweetheart, not jealous. Territorial. There's a difference.'

'I'm not a country, Nash,' she said coolly, but he could tell he'd rattled her. 'You can't invade me and stick up your flag.'

'I can do whatever I damn well please.'

He had hold of her wrist. He wasn't sure how that had happened. He just wanted answers. Despite everything he'd convinced himself about not wanting to dig any deeper, all of those possessive feelings had roared into life as she'd so casually admitted to a professional equestrian career.

She hid everything—and he'd thought *he* was the expert at keeping his private feelings under wraps. Lorelei could give him lessons.

'You're implying I sleep with men for money,' she said icily. 'I really don't think we'll be going any further, do you? Now, take your hands off me. I'm going home to bed.'

Nash shook his head.

'Are you going to release me?'

Her voice was very calm but he could see the betraying uncertainty in her expression. He was taken back to the first time he had seen her eyes—a little mountain deer quivering at his approach.

'Explain to me that party you had the other night.'

Lorelei frowned, shaking her head. 'Why do you care? What do you want from me, Nash? What is this about?'

'I want to understand you.' The words were almost prised from him. He couldn't understand where this seething frustration had come from but he needed answers.

The urge to rip her dress off her and have this out skin to skin in the sand, coupled with the need to protect her from herself, had him in a vortex of desire and self-loathing.

'Work!' she almost shouted at him. 'Just like you. Work!'

Her shoulders rose and fell.

'The CEO of the charity often asks me to host things,' she said jerkily. 'His wife finds it too oppressive. I was brought up to do these things.' She added the last almost wearily, 'By my *grand-maman.*'

'Who's dead?'

'Yes, she's dead!' Lorelei's voice lifted almost

on a wail. 'She's been dead two years, three months, five days!'

Nash stilled. There were tears behind Lorelei's eyes. She suddenly looked much younger and a little lost. Two years…It had to be around the time of her father's arrest. And she was still grieving.

She'd lost both her father and her grandmother.

'Is that why you still do it even though you can't afford it? Is that where the debts have sprung from?' He kept his voice low, not wanting to trigger those tears. He didn't know what he'd do if she began to cry.

Lorelei lowered her head. He could almost literally see her heart hammering. Her bare chest was so delicate—almost like a baby bird's. Guilt took a bite out of him. But he had to know if he was going to help her.

'Does this CEO bloke know about your problems with money?'

'I don't have a problem with money. I have a problem with paying my bills,' she said, lifting her chin a little aggressively. Baby bird or not, she was spitting like a cat. 'And, *non,* I don't care to share my private business with the world and his wife. Or you.'

She spun around and ran. He loped after her, hitting the automatic door release on the car.

The ten-minute drive back to the bungalow was tense, but it gave Nash time to think over all she'd said. His little eventer who couldn't manage her chequebook.

As they entered the dark house he asked, 'How long did you think you could hide it?'

'I wasn't hiding anything,' she rapped out, staccato-fashion. 'I was dealing with it. In my own way.'

'And how's that been working for you?'

'Well, pardon me,' she said, reeling around, 'but we're all not big, capable genius designers who can fix everything with the snap of our fingers!'

Nash stared down at her. 'What did you call me?'

'You heard—and I think your ego's big enough for me not to repeat it.'

He wanted to kiss her. Frame her lovely frustrated face and kiss her until she was his again.

'*Do* you want me to fix this for you?'

She frowned.

'Do you?' he repeated.

'You really don't know me at all, do you? You haven't even bothered to scratch the surface.'

Nash made a low sound of frustration. Didn't she understand he was going out on a limb for her here? He never pried too deeply into his lovers' lives. To do so invited intimacy, and he didn't do that. He did sex.

'How is it, Nash, that I know so much about you and you seem to know so little about me?'

'Sweetheart, only you know what you've read in the media—and most of that's crap.'

She narrowed her eyes at him like a cat, spun around and headed for the bedroom—then seemed to change her mind and bowled right back to him. 'Here's what I know. You're amazing. You're hardworking and driven and you have this shell that you need because you're in the public eye. But when you're with your friends you're different. You don't push your opinions or need other people to agree with you. You're just certain in a way I'll never be. I admire all those things about you.'

She was breathing hard, her eyes bright with repressed feeling. Nash tried not to engage but there she was, in his face.

'But all you admire about *me* is my world-class

ass—and don't even think about smiling, because as far as I'm concerned you can kiss it, Mr Racing Car Driver. I'm not waiting around for you to wake up to yourself.'

She really should have stopped after *amazing,* thought Nash as he stepped up to her, meshed his hand through her hair and brought his mouth down possessively on hers.

As if he'd lit a match next to an open petrol tank Lorelei ignited, surging against him, aggressive as he'd never felt her before. Even the first time she'd kissed him, when she'd taken the initiative, there had been a feminine reticence in her as if she needed to keep her protective barriers in place.

There were no barriers up now. The feel of her mouth moving desperately against his own made him crazy. Kissing her, hauling her with him, he staggered to the nearest flat surface—which happened to be one of the guest bedrooms. Nash would have laughed if he could at how eager he was—like a damn teenager, reefing down his trousers, with Lorelei making desperate noises as she cleaved to him, making it more difficult to actually shed any layers of clothing.

He slid his hands up her thighs, pooling her

long silken skirt, and remembered as his hand touched bare skin that she'd gone commando.

Thank God.

She whimpered and drew him to her, clamping her thighs around his lean hips. Her eyes were wide and what he saw there wasn't simply desire, it was anxiety.

'Lorelei?' He was so close to the edge, and yet she was looking at him as if she wasn't quite sure what was going on.

'Nash, I'm scared.' The words were almost wrenched from her. Her fingers were digging into his shoulders as if she was dangling off a cliff face, her bright troubled eyes fixed on his.

'Don't be.' He suddenly didn't feel all that secure himself, and that was a new experience. The words he found for her came from a deeper place inside him. 'I've got you.'

As if that were enough for her she lifted her mouth to his, shaking, a little wild, and her body came alive beneath his own in a way it never had before, coaxing him to take her. He only just remembered the condom. Deep inside her, he held on to his control by receding increments as she seemed unable or unwilling to let go. He felt her resistance not as a challenge but as a desperate uncertainty on her part. Her words came back at him. *You're just certain in a way I'll never be.*

He pressed his forehead to hers. 'Look at you,' he said, grazing her cheek, her mouth, her throat with his lips, moving slowly now. 'So strong, so wild. Do you remember when you threw that shoe at the traffic inspector?'

Lorelei gave a little start under him.

He brushed against her clitoris and she bucked. He did it again.

'Both shoes. I knew it then.'

'What—what did you know?'

'I'd never keep up.' He shifted his hips.

She made a sound—part murmur of approval, part moan.

'You stuck your finger in his face and read him the Riot Act.' He cupped her bottom. 'I thought you were going to get us arrested.'

She quaked against him. 'Sorry… I'm sorry.'

'No, no, don't be sorry,' he urged, moving harder inside her. 'Never be sorry. Do you remember when I took you back to the villa?' He angled his thrusts to reach higher. 'This—is what—I wanted—to do. Right there. In the Veyron.'

'Why?' she cried. 'Why didn't you?'

But she was already there.

'Stick shift,' he groaned as Lorelei's inner muscles clamped around him. He was grabbed and thrown down again and again, until his body convulsed uncontrollably against her and she clutched at him, riding out her own pleasure. It seemed as much his as hers, making sounds he only half recognised.

As he subsided heavily on top of her the chemical high kicked in and for several minutes he just held her, his chest pumping. He was conscious only of her trembling, responsive body cleaved to his—until he became aware something else was at play here. This wasn't just the euphoria of great sex. He could feel the connection with her still and didn't want to break it. He really didn't want to move, but he knew there was a risk if he didn't pull out of her, dispose of the condom.

It was as he began to sit up that he became aware she was making soft, helpless sounds. Insidious recognition reached down into his gut and grabbed hold of something he hadn't had to acknowledge in years.

The voice of his old man, telling him it was his fault, always his fault. To be a man and not a snivelling four-year-old boy.

He needed to hold her. That part of him that told him it was weakness that was at war with the man in him, who curved his hands around her slight, quaking shoulders, gathered her up in his arms and held her.

She turned her face into his shoulder and he experienced a surge of tenderness that threatened to further undo him. He was not accustomed to being gentle, but somehow he was, stroking the curls tumbling down the back of her neck, using his broad thumb to trace the curve of her ear, kissing her there because he needed to.

Except the face she lifted to his was not tear-streaked. Her amber eyes glowed; her cheeks were hot and flushed. She had never looked quite so beautiful, and she was smiling at him, softly laughing, her face haloed by all those silky fair curls.

'Stick shift.' She giggled as if she'd never heard anything funnier.

As he'd lost control he'd been listening not to Lorelei's tears but to her helpless, happy laughter as she came and came, and like a bolt of light-ning it hit him hard. With this woman, only with Lorelei, he felt like a conquering king.

* * *

Lorelei leaned across and gave Nash a lick of her ice cream.

She was sitting on the high sea wall and he was leaning against it between her legs, his back to her, his head just above her knees.

Beyond, fishermen were casting nets in the sea and local children ran splashing in the shoals, their happy voices punctuating the shriek of gulls, the occasional backfiring of a scooter, which seemed to be a popular method of transport, and the general hum of tourists and locals as the summer season ran out its course.

They had been exploring the tiny fishing village of Trou d'Eau Douce here on the east coast all morning, and lunch lay ahead, but Lorelei would have been perfectly content to stay exactly where they were. In the moment.

'This tourist route must be boring for you,' she said cheerfully, not sounding at all sorry.

'Yeah, I'm bored out of my mind,' Nash responded, giving her the benefit of a relaxed grin.

Lorelei didn't think she'd ever seen him this relaxed. They were supposed to be on a yacht with his friends, but this morning Nash had cancelled.

'Don't you have meetings? You haven't been

going to them. Isn't that the point of why we're here?' She had felt obliged to ask those questions, but her heart had been beating like hummingbird wings.

'The point is spending time with you,' he'd responded as if it were natural, and Lorelei had suddenly felt the world opening up around her into a thousand possibilities, all of them leading back to Nash.

He had forced secrets from her the other night, pushed past her fears and something important had cracked open in her, and instead of darkness only light had poured out.

He had made love to her all through the night until her body had felt like a map of Nash's voyages, each one leaving her feeling weightless and oddly free.

It was as if being here with him these last few days had unlocked those shackles of family and the past she'd been dragging around for so long. The thought of going back to how she had been seemed impossible now.

She was falling in love with him, and there could be no coming back from that. And if love was a voyage they were sailing into uncharted waters this morning.

Last night he had taken her hands and shown her the secrets of his body, almost intimidating in its muscular perfection but, like hers, telling stories.

He was marked all over with nicks and cuts, old scars from his years on the track that weren't always obvious until she touched him, ran her palms and fingertips over his back and hip, the long developed muscle of his quadriceps, and right there she had felt the groove in his flesh where he'd told her he'd had cartilage removed after a smash in Italy.

'Got adventurous on a corner and ended up upside down,' as he'd casually put it, 'with some wreckage in my leg.'

Yet last night on the beach outside a restaurant, when she had tried to ask him about himself, what drove him, he'd diverted her by hitting her most touchy subject: Raymond. In bed he had diverted again, by leading her directly to his physical scars, deftly hiding what lay beneath.

She wondered if he was always like this with women—stripping them bare of their secrets but managing to keep his own wound up nice and tight.

But she found she didn't want to think about

other women, his past, because it didn't matter to her. She wanted only to be in the moment, because she could trust that. Looking beyond, not knowing what was coming, instinctively frightened her.

'My *grandmaman* never let me buy ice creams when I was a little girl,' she confessed, licking the final scrap off the inner rim of the cone. 'She said ice cream should be eaten in a bowl with a spoon at a table. Preferably without your elbows touching any surfaces.'

'She sounds like an old dragon.'

'*Non,* she was always very sweet, just set in her ways. She raised me, you know, from when I was thirteen and started boarding school. I always came home to her in the holidays. She made it her mission in life to improve me.'

'What needed improving?'

'My manners. I was a total barbarian—you have no idea.'

She crunched the cone between her teeth.

Nash grinned and she offered him his own bite.

'Clearly still a barbarian.' She laughed, covering her mouth. 'I had to learn early how to behave myself in public. Grandmaman was quite well-known in our parts. She was photographed by Cecil Beaton in her day, you know. She was an amazing beauty.'

'I see where it comes from,' said Nash, those blue eyes scanning her face.

Lorelei shrugged off the compliment. 'Looks fade. She would have preferred to be an artist herself, but she was a wonderful patron. She drew artists, writers, musicians to our house. Quite a circle. Her third husband, my *grandpère,* left her a fortune and she set up the Aviary Foundation, a gallery in town and a charity to raise money for various causes. When the accident put paid to any hopes I had of a riding career she gave me new purpose, put me on the board of the Aviary where I've been ever since.'

'Your career, in effect?'

'*Ah, oui,* sometimes it feels that way. Although I've tried to keep the charity separate from my everyday life. It's not always easy.'

She paused, realising she'd gone wading into deeper waters. But she wanted to talk about this. She hadn't forgotten what he'd accused her of last night, or what he'd said back in Monaco when he'd cancelled their date.

'Despite what you think, Nash, I don't date the

men I deal with through the charity. I don't blur those lines.'

'Yeah…about that, Lorelei…'

He looked gratifyingly uncomfortable and it pleased a hurt little part of her.

'About that, Nash…?' she prompted.

'I was out of line. I apologise.'

'Do you?' Suddenly their easy camaraderie seemed forced. Her insecurities backed up in her throat.

She so wanted this man's understanding and approval, and it left her wide open to being hurt. All of a sudden she wasn't sure she could do that. But nor was she sure she had a choice any more.

Last night everything had changed for her.

'I was trying to work out how you lived your life. I was—' He broke off, as if he knew the more he said the deeper he'd be digging himself a hole.

Lorelei made a gesture of cessation. 'Perhaps we should just leave it at the apology.'

But his eyes flashed up and darkened on hers. 'I was jealous,' he said flatly.

Her heartbeat sped up. *'Ah, oui?'*

'Thinking about you with another man kills me.'

He said it as if it was being ripped out of him without anaesthetic, but he looked her in the eye and Lorelei found she was swaying a little with the impact of his words.

She lowered her lashes.

'Nothing to say, Lorelei?'

'Why, Nash, don't think about it, then.' She lifted her gaze and gave him a little smile.

'Not exactly what I was looking for,' he responded, but his eyes were warm.

Feeling a little breathless, she reached out and ran her fingers through his hair. 'That is nice to hear, Nash. Some not very nice things were intimated about me in the papers around the time of Raymond's trial. I think the journalists were just looking for dirt.'

'It sells papers,' said Nash grimly.

Oui, he would know. She was talking to a man who had spent more than a decade dodging the paparazzi.

'I hope I never have to go through that again. Five weeks in Paris for the trial, and every morning I opened the paper there would be another story.' Lorelei shuddered delicately.

Nash was frowning. She wondered what he was thinking. Had he read any of those stories? She didn't want to ask. She didn't want to think about it any more. But she did want to clear the air.

'All of these men I was supposed to be involved with—I was on Yurovsky's yacht last summer with at least fifteen other women, one of them his girlfriend at the time, and as for Damiano, I've known him since I was a teenager. It's never been romantic.'

'You don't need to explain your past to me,' he said roughly, but she could see the satisfaction curling like smoke in his eyes.

He was *jealous?*

'*Au contraire,* Nash, I've told you a great deal about my past and you've told me so little. I think you have a habit of privacy.'

'You want to hear about other women?'

Lorelei made a dismissive gesture. '*Eh, bien,* you will not be serious about this! Why don't you keep your important secrets, then?'

He leaned in and pushed her rogue curl behind her ear.

'What do you want to know, Lorelei?'

She brightened. 'We could start with something I asked you about last night—about your scars. You said you show them every time you race. What did you mean?'

The amusement dropped away from his expression and he rocked back on his heels.

'I know it's probably very complicated,' she persevered, 'but I'd like to know why you do what you do...'

'Complicated?' he said with a humourless smile. 'No, sweetheart, it's incredibly simple. It's in the blood. My old man, John Blue, worked in pit crews around the world and dragged us with him.'

'Ah, an international childhood.'

'Yeah, you could say that.'

He was quiet for a moment, but Lorelei waited. She sensed she'd just glimpsed the tip of an almighty iceberg.

'Mum walked out when I was barely more than a baby. Couldn't take the lifestyle, couldn't take the old man. Can't blame her.'

He turned away from her, shoving his hands into his pockets, bunching his shoulders.

'She left us boys with Dad,' he said, looking away down the beach as if scanning for something. 'He was a drunk and a bully and he made our lives a living hell. Until one day when Jack— my older brother—was big enough to climb behind the wheel of a car and he started us both rally driving. Jack was good, but I was better.'

She didn't quite understand. 'You raced for your *papa?*'

'No, I raced in spite of my old man.' His voice was taut and stripped of emotion. 'He had world-class dreams and I was going to fulfil them for him. The minute I signed with Ferrari I cut contact with him.'

Lorelei suppressed a shiver. He hadn't shown this side to her. She imagined it was this single mindedness that had made him so very good at what he did and a very wealthy man.

'You took your revenge?' she said quietly, uncertain as to how she felt about that.

'No, I survived.'

It was a terse statement, to the point, and it chilled her to the bone.

'You didn't abandon your old man,' he said suddenly, meeting her eyes, and she could see he'd shut down again, 'I admire that.'

'Non.' The negative was pushed from her instinctively. She rejected his statement with her entire body. 'Don't admire me. My mother wasn't there for me either, but my father didn't drink or make my life hell—at least not on purpose. He

loved me. How could I abandon him? I couldn't abandon someone I love.'

Nash was watching her as if her words were flicks of a knife.

'Good,' he said with finality, and she knew the subject was closed, 'I'm glad he loves you. You deserve that, Lorelei.'

Meaning he didn't? Lorelei wanted to offer him something, but she had a strong feeling whatever she did in this moment would be rejected. He was a man driven by demons and it was all too possible she had come too late into his life to make any difference at all.

With a sudden movement Nash bounded up onto the sea wall beside her, offering her his hand. Standing over her, he was once more the solid, take-charge guy who made the world seem a less chaotic, threatening place when she was with him.

'Enough of the past. I want to show you the mountains this afternoon. We'll take the Jeep up.'

Later that evening over dinner she asked him the question that had been bothering her most. 'That accident you were in, in Italy, is that why you got out of the sport?'

Nash shook his head. 'You'd think so, but no.' His voice was quiet and deep and sure. The rose candlelight cut into the restaurant walls, lining his dark head in gold. 'My take on it is I don't have any dependants. If I killed myself racing at least I'd leave the world doing something I loved.'

Lorelei almost choked on her mouthful of wine, a little stunned by his matter-of-factness. 'That's a terrible thing to say.'

'I'm not planning on careening off the track any time soon, Lorelei.'

'No, but—' She broke off helplessly, wondering if he actually knew how empty he had made his life sound. 'What about your brother Jack?' she prompted.

Nash said nothing, began cutting into his steak.

'What about me?' The moment the words passed her lips she couldn't believe she'd been so gauche. 'What I mean to say is, if anything happened to you I'd be heartbroken.' She gave him a small smile to lighten the impact.

He reached for his iced water. 'I'll keep that in mind.'

Lorelei had the urge to rub the spot in her chest that had gone suddenly cold.

'Something must have made you stop,' she said, her voice a lot less confident.

He put down his glass. 'My brother Jack is an alcoholic, like the old man. He let his business slide, lost his wife, gambled away his life. He thought he had nothing more to live for. Six years ago I walked into a hospital room in Sydney and I barely recognised him. I'd been racing profes- sionally for eight years, and I'd been back once.'

Nash met her eyes. 'His ex-wife told me I was to blame. Jack always wanted the career, but I was the one who got the talent. So I quit racing. I moved back to Sydney and I lived with him for a year. Got his business back on its feet, went every day to AA with him and made sure he was okay. I owed it to him. He got me to university. He's my brother. And he hates me.'

'But why?'

'The talent and the luck. To my old man I was a meal ticket, and my brother was convinced I stole what should have been his. In my family no- body works. The joke is I've worked hard all my life to get where I am. That's what I do. I work. I came back to Europe and I sold the design for Blue 11, and part of the reason I did it was be- cause I wanted to show them it was more than luck, more than being able to hold a car on the road at speed.'

His expression was grim. 'It should have been enough for me, but it wasn't. I love to race. And now I don't have to prove anything. To the old man, to Jack, even to myself. I don't want to lose it a second time.'

Lorelei was quiet. Finally she said, 'Hence the comeback?'

'You picked up on that the other night at dinner?'

'It was hard not to. I was at the table, Nash.'

He put his hands palm-down on the table, giving her a wry smile. 'Have I ever told you, you do have a world-class ass, Ms St James?'

'Several times,' she replied dryly, dabbing at the tears in the corners of her eyes, then offering up her most beguiling smile. He deserved it after that. 'I think you should take me home and I'll show it to you.'

Nash pushed back his chair, raised his hand for the cheque.

Lorelei lay with her head on his chest, her mind full of the story he had told her. She knew it was selfish, but she couldn't help wishing he wasn't

staging this comeback—because it was going to
have repercussions on their fledgling relationship.

'Why now, Nash? Why race now?'

His voice was heavy, relaxed. 'Like I told you,
I started out racing in spite of my father. Now I
race for myself.'

'But why now in particular?' she pursued.

'I don't know.' He yawned. 'At the risk of
sounding New Agey, I've been feeling a lack in
my life and I know racing will fill that.'

'What sort of lack?'

Nash chuckled. 'Not the sort you're imagin-
ing, Lorelei.'

A little frustrated, she lifted her chin. 'You
don't know what I'm thinking.'

'Yeah...' his smile was lazy '...I do. I'm thirty-
four. All anyone's going to be asking over the
coming months before I start winning any flags
is whether it's an early midlife crisis.'

'You're confident of winning?'

He gave her that very male look she was already familiar with. It was a redundant question. He was confident about everything, and he
always won.

She sat up. 'During the early months of my rehabilitation the thing that got me out of bed was the desire to get back in the saddle. It was only when I realised I couldn't go back to competitive riding that I found the emptiness resided not in the fulfilment of a dream but in the absence of anything else in my life.'

There was a long silence.

'So what's in your life now?' he asked, his voice deceptively lazy.

But Lorelei knew him well enough to catch the watchfulness in those blue eyes viewing her from beneath heavy lids.

You.

The rush of feeling overwhelmed her. She wanted to be enough for him.

She wanted to stand in for racing.

She wanted him to realise what an extraordinary man he was, and for once to stop pushing himself.

She wanted a great deal she probably couldn't have.

'I have my work,' she said diffidently.

'Yeah, the charity.'

'No, my horses…' she began with a little frown.

'You have horses?'

'*Oui,* two, I stable them at Allards.'

'So you still ride?'

'Whenever I can.' She hesitated, then went on the offensive. 'So what are you lacking in *your* life, Nash?'

'Me?' He looked amused. 'I'm just easily bored.'

'I'll have to come up with some ways of keeping you from being bored, then,' she said softly, and slid forward over him, her curls falling down to brush over his chest in the way he liked. His eyes met hers, and all that banked heat made the blood pool in her thighs and pelvis. 'I've got a few ideas.'

She knew how to make a man want her, trip over his feet to get to her, but it had never been about that with Nash. From the moment he had put his hand on her shoulder outside the hotel and told her he would handle it, rushed to her rescue like a valiant knight, she'd been off-centre with him. She had always looked after herself, knowing all too well how unreliable men could be. She had given Nash access to the vulnerable heart of hers and made him her lover, and right now she knew there should be more.

For the first time in her life she wanted more.

'Isn't this comeback supposed to be hush-hush?' she asked

He cupped her bottom. 'I think I'm safe.'

Lorelei kissed him. He was telling her he trusted her, that he accepted her right to know and she had his respect.

'Besides,' he said complacently as she kissed her way down his body, her bare bottom resting back on his thighs, 'we're releasing a timed leak on Monday. By Wednesday the media will be all over it.'

Lorelei felt as if he'd yanked a rug out from under her.

Her head came up. He wasn't saying he trusted her at all. He was just saying the timing made it irrelevant. She tried to ignore the crumpling in her chest.

'What's happening Wednesday?' she asked, feeling a little sidelined.

'A press conference,' he replied calmly, stroking her thighs, 'and then lockdown.'

'What's lockdown?'

'Training.'

'And then what?'

'The circuit.'

'A lot of travel?'

'For the next year.'

He sat up, and she gave a gasp as he flipped

her onto her belly and began placing hot kisses down her spine, over the rounded curves of her bottom.

'Perhaps I can fly in?' she suggested, feeling a little stunned.

'I'd enjoy that,' he said, tracing one quivering buttock.

'Would you?' she said a little sharply.

Nash put his mouth to her ear. 'Your visits would be most welcome.'

She waited for him to ask her to go with him. He didn't.

Nash took the steps by threes, coming out of the darkness into the bright light spilling down the front of the bungalow. He was impatient to get back to Lorelei.

This afternoon they'd driven back to the bungalow around dusk. Nash had never felt less like a boys' night, but he knew he'd been fairly difficult to pin down, given he was spending all his time with Lorelei, and there were ends to tie up and other people involved in this. He had responsibilities.

'Two hours, tops,' he'd told her, 'and then I take you out to dinner.'

She had smiled softly, a little sad, he knew, because of what he'd told her last night. He had his reasons, and it had not been easy, but she needed to understand racing came first.

He found the bungalow empty and for a strange moment his insides hollowed out.

She was gone….

This was how it would feel next week, and the week after that, and after that.

He made a frustrated sound, slamming the door. He was behaving like a green kid. There was no reason why he couldn't keep seeing her on a casual basis. A few nights here and there when he was in town, perhaps flying her out when he was working. He was capable of cleaning this up, keeping everything locked down.

Then he noticed the doors onto the deck were wide open. He relaxed. This at least was familiar. She was outside—probably on the beach. Then he spotted it: a piece of white paper weighted under a rock at the top of the steps leading down to the beach. There was another one on the bottom step. He hesitated, then smiled to himself.

He had found four paper signals when he caught sight of her on the shore. He stood at the edge of the clearing. She was clearly waiting for him, because the moment she saw him she lifted her sheer kaftan.

He stopped dead.

She was wearing one of those tiny bikinis the boutique had interpreted as adequate beachwear. Adequate, Nash countered, if the beach was private and no other man was going to see her in it.

She reached behind her and untied the strap of the top.

A sudden surge of instinct had him doing a quick scan of their surroundings, aware his might not be the only pair of eyes on this little show. There was nothing but the private beach, the rustle of the wind in the palms and tropical undergrowth and the murmur of the water on the shore.

Lorelei was peeling off the bikini bottoms, utterly unselfconscious. He watched as she lifted her arms above her head, moving with lithe grace as she stretched sinuously, seeming to be enjoying the warm breeze moving over her skin. There was a full moon and at this angle she looked to be reaching for it with both hands.

She spun around, her head sank back and she began to dance.

Nash swore his heart stopped. He knew her body—he'd explored every inch of her firm, tanned flesh—but in this moment he almost didn't recognise her. Because he saw something more—the instinctive sensuality that was a part of her, her incredible naturalness and her acceptance not only of her body but of the cards life had dealt her.

Why had he not seen this before? The answer was there. He'd been blind.

His desire for her was suddenly a living flame inside him.

He strode down the beach towards her.

She continued to turn and glide, and when he was mere feet from her she slipped away with a soft laugh, running nimbly down to the surf.

Nash didn't hesitate. He stripped off his shoes, shirt, trousers, boxers and strode down to plunge recklessly into the cool draw of the ocean. The water was inky, but the moonlight cast enough light for him to see Lorelei, still now, as gentle waves broke at her hips.

She laughed as he caught her around the waist, dragged her down into the water with him.

A wave smacked against his back and he caught her mouth with his and tasted salt and woman. *His* woman. Lorelei.

She licked her way into his mouth, winding those slim arms around his neck, her slick body riding against his in the water. Her long legs wound around his, and he lifted her, his sex nudging hers. She was wet and hot and welcoming, and he was surprised the water around them didn't sizzle with the heat they were generating between them.

She was like some pagan priestess, initiating him into this rite, uninhibited and demanding as a great goddess should be, taking and offering in equal measure.

He rode deep into her body, the sway of the tide pulling them this way and that, making achieving a rhythm almost impossible. Yet the ocean held their bodies aloft and his climax eventually pulled him into a vortex of perfect symmetry with her. Lorelei pulsed around him, and if he was a fanciful man—which he was not—he would have said it was like flying.

He eventually carried her out of the water and up to the beach, where he wrapped her in a towel and took her inside. She was shivering and laughing as he dumped them both under the shower, with warm water cascading down. He washed her hair and then rubbed some of the lemon-scented liquid into his own.

She leaned against him as he rinsed her off, and he was struck all over again by how delicate she was. That feeling of possession he'd been nurturing this week roared into life. He didn't want to let her go.

It was never supposed to have been more than a few days out of time—a last indulgence before the weeks of intensive training that lay ahead. He couldn't have known she would get under his skin. Women came and went. Yet as he tumbled her into their bed he knew part of Lorelei would always stay with him.

His chest felt tight, but he knew he would get past this. He had life lessons to draw on in how to master his own emotions and make them serve him. Painful lessons, learned by a small boy too young to really understand what was happening in his life, always looking for someone to cling to, always being punished for it. The constant cycle of confusion.

There was nothing confusing about the life he had grown up to lead. Everything was compartmentalised. Everything had its place.

Including this. Including Lorelei.

Tomorrow he would be flying back to Monaco and straight into the press conference, a show race for Eagle in Lyon, and then training. He wasn't ready. He had been doing too much thinking about this beguiling woman in his arms and not enough about the job.

The irony was, if he was given another week he'd spend it all with her.

But he'd never put a woman before the job.

Like his parents, he knew how to be ruthless to achieve his ends.

Lorelei was dreaming. In her dream she was walking down a long corridor. There were doors on either side of her, stretching as far as she could see.

As she passed they would open.

There was her mother. She was young—as Lorelei recalled her in her earliest years—holding out a doll with long golden curls that bore a marked resemblance to the child she had been before she cut off her hair. Another door opened on her father, Raymond, as she had last seen him, rigid in a suit, his back to her. Finally there was *Grandmaman,* holding out money in one hand and a tiny miniature of the villa in the other.

Lorelei could feel the constriction growing in her body. She was moving faster. Hands were coming out to snatch at her skirt, her ankles, demanding things of her until she thought she would go crazy. And then she heard a deep, certain voice saying her name. 'Lorelei.' She stepped into his arms and the walls of the dream fell away. She was held poised in midair in the strongest pair of arms imaginable.

'Nash.' She clung to him and knew she was home, would always be safe.

He wouldn't let go. Which meant she *could* let go…

Lorelei gasped, coming awake in a bath of perspiration. Nash was leaning over her in the dark. He gently stroked the hair back from her eyes.

'Go to sleep. His voice was deep and sleep roughened. 'It was just a nightmare.'

'Oui,' she murmured croakily, and closed her eyes.

For a long while she lay awake, with Nash's arm pinning her, his body curved around hers like a bulwark against uncertainty.

She felt a little *triste.* It could have been because of the fast-fading dream but was probably because they were going back to Monaco tomorrow.

But it wasn't the villa or her debts that filled her

horizon, it was the man beside her, who appeared not to be sleeping either, although his chest rose and fell steadily.

She burrowed in a little closer.

I've fallen in love with this man, she thought, framing it like a statement and waiting to feel the panic it should open up inside her.

All those fears of dependency, of being left behind, of not being loved back.

None came.

She curved her body trustingly into his and closed her eyes. She was back in the ocean with him, certain of this one thing: *this has been as close to flying as I've ever come.*

CHAPTER THIRTEEN

'LORELEI, we need to talk.'

According to the flight screen they were twenty minutes out of Nice.

Lorelei removed her ear buds and looked up. Nash had been hooked into a laptop for the better part of an hour, which was why they hadn't been sitting together.

Or at least she told herself that was why, but she had been telling herself a great many things since boarding his plane. If he was being a little distant this morning she assumed he was thinking about what he was flying back into. She certainly was.

He was a famous man, about to reignite that fame, and there were consequences for her. She would be foolish to discount them.

But when she looked at him everything fell away, leaving only what she felt for him: a tremulous sort of tenderness mingled with a longing to have this in her life.

He dropped into the seat beside her, stretching out his long legs, but there was nothing casual about the expression on his face.

'You look ominous,' she said lightly.

'Do I?' He looked at her, his eyes cool. 'I'm going into lockdown tomorrow. That's going to have ramifications on my personal life.'

His personal life? She guessed that meant her. She moistened her lips.

'I see.'

Did she see? Lorelei curled the fingers of one hand around her music device instead of around his hand.

Why, all of a sudden, couldn't she reach for his hand?

Yesterday she wouldn't even have thought about it. She wouldn't have had to. Whenever he was beside her he held her hand.

'I gather it will limit the time we can spend together?' Her voice held none of the turmoil suddenly swirling in her belly.

'I'll be training intensively and then I hit the circuit.' Nash spoke matter-of-factly. 'This hasn't happened at a propitious time. I wish it could be different, but it can't.'

Lorelei had never thought about what it would

be like to jump from a plane without a parachute. She imagined the landing would feel something like this.

There were so many things she could say. *I don't understand. Please explain yourself more clearly. Don't do this. Please don't do this....*

But he was doing it. She looked into his hard eyes and knew beyond a shadow of a doubt he would do this to her.

'I don't want you to feel tied to me in any way.'

Lorelei tried to sit up but every bone in her body felt broken. Still, she had to get up. She couldn't just sit here, stunned.

'It wouldn't be fair to you.'

From a long way away she was hearing an echo from the past. It was her father, explaining why she couldn't live with him any more, that she was to go to her grandmother. She'd been thirteen years old. She hadn't understood then. She had cried until she threw up.

But she understood now. She was a grown woman. She had lived in the world, had been swept away by feelings that fed her soul, and he had enjoyed some recreational sex.

'How good of you to explain it all to me,' she said, her voice more throaty than usual. 'I suppose there is a reason we didn't have this conversation several days ago?'

He was watching her stone-faced. 'Things have changed. Several days ago I didn't know we would need to.'

'I see—and what has changed for you?'

'I didn't realise we'd be going any further than Mauritius.'

She knew he was right. She hadn't thought beyond Mauritius, either. She'd just assumed everything would fall into place.

'Lorelei, I know you've invested some emotions in our time together,' he said almost carefully. 'When we flew out I made some assumptions.'

'Ah, oui.' She clutched her music device and in that moment wished it were a weapon. 'All the men I was supposed to have fleeced.' The words stuck to the roof of her mouth.

'Assumptions about myself,' he growled.

For the first time she looked at him properly. He didn't look like a man feeding her a line. He looked like Nash. Tense, brooding, not wanting to hurt her, but tearing her apart all the same.

After all, Lorelei, it's not his fault he's not in love with you. You made that little bed all on your own.

But he had been there with her. All the way.

'You're an extraordinary woman, Lorelei, and you deserve a lot better than a man like me.'

And just like that it was over.

'Apparently I do,' she said woodenly, hearing her voice as if it were coming from a long way off. 'I really don't know what to say.'

For the first time since he'd sat down beside her Nash looked unsure, as if they had taken a wrong turn somewhere and he was looking for the best way to circumvent the route.

'I don't necessarily want to end it, Lorelei. All I am saying is there are difficulties involved. I'll be gone for long periods and my focus will be on the job.'

All the cold inside her chest pushed its way up into her mind. She welcomed it.

'I'm saying I wouldn't want you to feel committed to me.'

Lorelei blinked. Her eyes were the only part of her face she could move.

'You really are a complete bastard, aren't you?'

Those intense blue eyes flashed up, hard as agate, but his voice was soft as he acknowledged heavily, 'Yeah.'

What more was there to say?

She didn't know how to fight for this. How did you fight for something that had to be given freely? She didn't understand him. She'd thought she did. She had seen in him from the very first such solidity. He had seemed impervious to the turmoil in her life, a strong hand she could hold as she righted herself.

So she had opened up her heart to him, had thought she understood him, but it was clear she knew nothing at all.

Anger and rage and sorrow all rolled through her in an almighty wave and she thought if it crashed now the emotions would drag her under.

She had to be strong. *Stronger than him.*

'What happened to you? Who did this to you?'

He actually flinched as she said the words. He stood up, those big shoulders that held up the world suddenly a little heavier, his expression almost remote.

'I've got a job to do, Lorelei, and relationships have never been my strong suit.'

No, me neither....

She actually felt too stunned to fully process what had happened. It was only when they landed on the tarmac and she spotted the limo that confusion set in.

What was she supposed to do? Was he taking her back to town? To the villa? Oh, *Dieu,* she couldn't get into the villa. She gulped a deep, sustaining breath. She needed to calm down. She needed to stop standing around waiting for him to call the shots.

Taxi. She needed a taxi.

Nash said, almost formally, 'The car is for you. It will take you into town. I'll take the Veyron.'

For a moment she considered refusing, but what was the point?

'Ainsi soit-il.' So be it.

'The car will take you back to my apartment. You can stay there until you get back on your feet.'

He had to be kidding.

As if anticipating her reaction, he said, 'You need a roof over your head.'

'I do not think that is your concern any longer, Mr Blue.' Her voice was croaky, as if she'd been yelling for a very long time.

'Let me do this for you,' he said quietly.

The bastard.

She stepped up to him, looked him in the eye. 'Why on earth didn't you just leave me on the doorstep that morning after? If all you wanted was a one-night stand you could have left it there. I didn't ask for you to take me to Mauritius. But I damn well deserve better than being dumped fifteen minutes after we land.'

It was good to say it, and to say it with some control, but she knew she wasn't just raging at Nash. She was raging at her dear, feckless father, who had rescued her from her absent mother's apartment in New York all those years ago, only to neglect her and dump her on his mother, who for all her good intentions had been a difficult and sometimes ferocious taskmaster.

She deserved to be loved and accepted for who she was, not what others expected her to be.

Nash looked her in the eye and said, 'Yeah, you do.'

It was that resigned acceptance of her anger and his role in her pain that left her with nowhere to go. He was behaving as if it was all inevitable.

As if he didn't have a choice.

But he did. Couldn't he see that? Surely he could see that?

She'd fought like a tiger to regain full mobility after her accident, she'd stood by Raymond through his trial and all the scathing publicity, and she'd struggled like a fish in a net to hold on to the villa these past months.

But she couldn't make this man fight for her.

Turning away, she said softly, 'Nash, do you have any feelings for me at all?'

'Lorelei, of course I do.' He jaw was so rigid it was a wonder he could speak.

She took a deep breath.

'*Bon,*' she said forcefully, and pushed past him. 'In that case I don't ever want to see you again.'

She stepped into the limo.

'Take her wherever she wants to go,' she heard him say to the driver.

In the car Lorelei blocked the oncoming truck-load of pain by opening her cell and regrouping.

She checked her client list for next week and sent off a text to Gina's mother to bump up her appointment for this afternoon. Work, rules and structure. She had never needed it so much as right now. She sent a text to her solicitor, asking for an appointment, which gave her a vague feeling of asserting a little control over events. Finally she scrolled through her address book, turning over in her mind which one of her friends she could ask for a bed.

In the end she sent a text to Simone. A million miles away in Paris.

Please come. I need you.

Then she closed her eyes and decided the tears that were building inside her really had no place right now. She would hold them until she was alone. And with that she realised for the first time in two years she was once more in complete control of her actions.

Nash was about to throw the keys for valet parking outside the hotel when suddenly he knew he wouldn't be going inside. It had only taken a couple of phone calls on the way down to have information regarding the lien on Lorelei's loan sent through, and in an hour the locks would be taken off her house. But somehow it wasn't enough.

He reached into his pocket and palmed his cell, dialled the limo. 'Where did you drop her, mate?'

He had a press conference. He had a training schedule ahead. He needed to let her go. Instead he leapt back in the car and gunned the engine.

He'd driven past, but never been inside the equestrian centre. There had never been a reason. He gave her name at the desk and the wide-eyed girl told him Lorelei should be in the arena and asked did he need an escort? She was free.

'I'm sure I can find it,' he replied with a slight smile, and followed the arrows.

What in the hell did he think he was doing? Better question: why had she come here? Straight here? Who was she meeting? He couldn't fathom the growing jealousy in him.

The first thing that hit him was the odour of manure and horse. So far, so expected. He jogged lightly down the steps of the stadium seating, scanning as he went. There were horses being worked in the domed arena. He recognised Lorelei. She was unmistakable, leaping a bay gelding over barriers. It was a breathtaking sight. Her grace and ability was fully on show.

He sank down slowly onto one of the bench seats.

Presently she drew alongside another rider, and that was when he noticed something else. The young girl on the smaller horse had a prosthesis on both her right arm and leg. Lorelei was showing her how to guide her horse.

An arrow-backed middle-aged woman sitting nearby looked at him with interest. She was the only other person within earshot.

She leaned back. 'Lorelei runs our programme here for disabled young people. She's a superb trainer. If you're interested I can set up an appointment, but I have to warn you she's in demand. There's a waiting list.'

Nash gave the woman a polite nod and settled back.

He didn't know what he was feeling.

But, my God, she was magnificent.

She looked like a queen in the saddle.

He remembered what she had told him about her two years of rehabilitation. He'd just assumed she'd given up. When he knew better than most what made someone a gifted athlete was that drive. Why hadn't he realised she would take that same drive and rechannel it?

It was what he had done.

The trappings of fame and success for him had become the bells and whistles people paid attention to. But he'd earned it with hard work and focus. Yet he'd completely discounted that when he'd looked at Lorelei. He'd just seen bells and whistles, a beautiful blonde bauble. Why?

Feelings shifted like tectonic plates in his chest. Why hadn't he asked more questions? Why hadn't he seen this in her? She wasn't weak. She was strong. It made sense that she would pick herself up and start all over again. And she'd do the same with that bloody house of hers.

However she'd accumulated those debts, there would be a good reason.

And he intended to find out.

Nash wasn't sure how long he sat and watched. He only knew when he emerged into the late afternoon he wanted to smash something. When he returned to his car his cell was throwing up a volley of messages.

The press conference.

He hit redial. 'John, I'm on my way.'

He walked into a conclave of cameras and the relief of his Eagle teammates. He sat down, put his hands either side of the mike and said calmly, 'Ladies, gentlemen—sorry to keep you waiting. I'm driving for Eagle next year.'

A volley of questions came at him. He took a few, then fielded the rest, scrolling through his phone.

He knew tomorrow there'd be copy on how Nash Blue had been so bored at his own press conference he'd seemed more interested in playing with his phone. At another time it would have amused him. But right now he didn't care about the press, the public or even the Eagle reps, who seemed more than adequately able to handle this without him.

He got up and walked out into the empty carpeted corridor.

'Mike,' he said with deceptive casualness to his genius PA, 'I've got a few leads I need chased up.' He asked for all the pertinent information about Raymond St James's trial and his creditors.

John Cullinan stepped into the hall. 'Nash, man, are you in this or not?'

'Yeah.' Nash pocketed his cell. He'd done all he could for the moment. 'I'm in.'

Sitting on the little red couch in a twin room at the Hotel de Paris, Lorelei shook her head over the paperwork the bank had given her.

'So let me get this straight,' said Simone, mixing coffee. 'He's opened up negotiations with the bank for you, covered your outstanding mortgage payments and is acting as guarantor for the next six months?'

'*Oui*, it appears so.'

'Is that legal?'

'If I give the bank my signature.'

Simone stopped stirring. 'If? *If*?'

'I can't accept this, Simone. Not now.'

'You're going to accept it, *chère,* if I have to tie you up and carry you down there myself. He must be feeling a cartload of guilt to be doing this.'

'*Non,* it's just Nash—the way he is.' Generous. Always so generous with his time and his money…and his brother. He'd given up everything for a year for his brother. He'd given up his racing career for his brother.

He deserved to have another chance.

Lorelei found her breathing had become scratchy.

Like Simone. Who had flown down immediately from Paris, leaving her children with her husband and taking a leave of absence from her high-powered job. To make coffee, offer a kind shoulder and listen.

You did those things for the people you loved.

But he didn't love her or he wouldn't have let her go.

Simone came and set a mug down in front of her.

'He's racing tomorrow in Lyon. We could go. You could speak to him about this.'

Lorelei shook her head vigorously.

Simone gave her an old-fashioned look. 'Do

you know what I think, *chère?* This man loves you. He's just having a few problems working out how to show it.'

'Don't, Simone. You have no idea how many times I heard all my stepmothers and their girl-friends talking like this. *He's this way because he's a man. He's this way because you make him like this.* In the end he's this way because it's who he is. It's who he wants to be. Nash wants to race cars, he wants to win and he puts work above everything.'

Lorelei released a huge sob of a breath.

'All my life that's how it's been. *Papa* put his women ahead of me. *Grandmaman* put the char-ity ahead of me. I'm not mooning over a man who thinks oil and grease and speed outweigh my love.'

'You're in love with him.' Simone sat down beside her.

'That's what you got out of my little speech?'

Simone shook her head with a smile. 'Isn't it all that matters in the end, *cherie?*'

Was it all that mattered?

Lorelei lay awake, staring out at the night.

Her father would say, *Oui, but of course. L'amour is everything.*

But Raymond had never really loved anybody in his life but himself, with a little corner of his heart reserved for her.

She deserved so much more. Everyone deserved to be loved wholeheartedly and for themselves. A sob made its way up through her body, leaving her shaken, but still she couldn't cry.

She loved Nash, really loved him, but she felt battered. He had left her behind, he didn't love her back, and here she was—so very, very dependent on him.

Except for one thing.

The villa.

He could have gifted it to her. The meaningless gesture of an excessively wealthy man. He hadn't. He had chosen instead to take the pressure off her with the gift of time. Time to think. Time to make a decision about what she really wanted to do. It also enabled her to envisage a time when she could pay him back.

He knew her well enough to know it was the only gift she wouldn't throw back in his face.

Lorelei rolled onto her back.

Mon Dieu, he hadn't made her dependent. He had made her strong again.

In every way.

Lorelei bolted up in bed.

She flung open the other bedroom door and the little bedside light flickered on as Simone sat up groggily.

'How long will it take me to drive to Lyon?'

'Three hours, give or take.' Simone yawned. 'Why?'

Lorelei bit her lip. 'I'm going to do what I should have done on that plane. Fight for him.'

Simone gave her a wavery smile. 'Should I expect to see you on the news tomorrow night, throwing punches at track girls?'

It was a gentle reminder not to overreact.

Except what had Nash told her? Not to be sorry, never to be sorry.

'It's always a possibility.'

CHAPTER FOURTEEN

IT WAS race day.

Nash continued to scan the documents emailed to his smartphone. Raymond St James had quite a list of creditors.

Lifting his eyes from the bright screen, for a moment all Nash could see was Lorelei, locked out of her beloved home, trying desperately to steer him away, to hide the truth of her situation, only admitting, when forced, 'I have had some debts.'

Some debts.

'Nash, man, you're cutting it fine.'

He dumped the phone and dragged up the zipper on his fire-retardant suit, pulled the face mask on and reached for his helmet.

The sound of the crowd, the smell of gasoline fumes, the whir of his car being readied usually pushed up his adrenaline levels. But this afternoon he didn't need any help with that.

His heart was pounding, he was sweating inside the hot suit, but he knew how to switch off and do his job.

He'd raced all over the globe for a decade.

He'd won; he'd lost. Mostly he'd won.

He usually knew the outcome before he got in the car. He studied the field, he knew his car and he applied logic and ability and allowed for that two per cent of unpredictability that lay in any race.

It was that two per cent that was on his mind—and it had nothing to do with the race.

As he ripped across the finish line outside Lyon the fact that he took little pleasure in the win didn't detract from the roar of the crowd. Slinging himself out of the car, he embraced Alain Demarche and Antonio Abruzzi in turn. Shook hands with a couple of guys from the pit crew and mounted the podium.

He was stepping off amidst champagne and track girls when he saw her.

She was standing with Nicolette Delarosa. She was wearing blue jeans and a simple green shirt and her hair was a halo around her piquant face. But, most tellingly, a lanyard dangled around her neck.

He focused on the lanyard, knowing then that this wasn't some fantasy apparition. She was real. Heart thumping, he moved away from the podium but the crowd had already swallowed her up.

He shouldered his way through and grabbed one of the security guards forming a phalanx around him.

'There'll be a '55 Sunbeam Alpine in the VIP car park. Can you hold on to it until I get out?'

'Sure thing.'

'The woman who owns it will kick up a fuss. Make sure she's treated with respect.'

'Absolutely. Great race, man.'

'Thanks.'

Let her be there. If she wasn't he'd grab a car and drive every mile back to Monaco and fetch her.

He hadn't wanted to race today. All he had wanted to do was go and fetch her back. But he had a job to do. A lot of people were relying on him—as always. You couldn't escape responsibility for others. Lorelei had never tried. Her compassionate humanity humbled him.

She had hidden so much behind those charming mannerisms. What he had read as light-heartedness and frivolity were her coping mechanisms. He'd got it all wrong.

How in the hell had he got it so wrong?

In the bungalow the night he'd confronted her about hiding things she'd accused him of not knowing her at all, of not trying to know her.

She'd been right.

He hadn't wanted to look at what was shouting in his face. He'd been so damned determined to keep to his single-minded plan to race that he'd been willing to sacrifice this extraordinary chance he'd been given to love and be loved to his own selfish need to prove himself. To prove his old man was wrong. He wasn't weak, a snivelling kid who drove people away with his demands for love and attention, the innocent child who had reached instinctively for love and been denied it. So he'd learned to deride his own needs, and when Lorelei had come along, he hadn't had a clue how to even *begin* loving her.

Yet he did. Her compassion and her humanity had torn into those barriers he'd raised, yet still he'd gone back for more.

It had always been there when they made love, from the very first night, and he'd seen it when she danced on the beach—the acceptance in her body of who she was.

Her acceptance of *him*.

Come be with me. Let me show you how to love me, how to love yourself.

He closed his eyes, took a deep, sustaining breath, and knew his life had just taken a sudden irrevocable turn. For the better.

He was in his civvies and to his surprise Lorelei was just sitting on the bonnet of her car. Not kicking, not scratching, not a thrown shoe in sight. She was chatting casually with three security guys, who stood around looking more interested in making an impression than doing their job.

The guys evaporated with polite nods as Nash approached. Lorelei leaned back, angling her body at him. The old playful pose dragged him back to the first time he'd met her, when she'd put on that little show and he'd lost his head over her.

'I thought I dreamed you up,' he said, his voice suddenly rather hoarse.

'Are you in the habit of doing that?'

'Lately? Yeah. All the time.'

She slid off the bonnet of the car and stood

before him, suddenly not so sure of herself, her face solemn.

'I'm not Jack,' she said.

He went still.

'And I'm grateful for the time with the villa, but I'm not your rescue package, Nash Blue.'

He bowed his head.

'I know that, Lorelei,' he said in a thickened voice. 'I saw you at the equestrian centre. The day we got back I followed you.'

'You followed me? I didn't see you.'

'You were training a young girl with a prosthesis. I had no idea.' He stepped towards her, aching to take her in his arms. 'Why didn't you tell me?'

Lorelei hesitated. 'I don't know. I could say it was because it didn't come up, but the truth is…' Her voice died away. She shook her head. 'I'm not proud of it, but I wanted to hold something back from you because I sensed you were holding so much back from me.'

He nodded slowly. 'Fair enough. But you have to know when I got the big picture everything I'd told myself about my feelings for you came crashing down. I didn't want to love you, Lorelei, and so I told myself you could never be anything but another person I'd have to bail out.'

'In the end you did,' she said in a strangled voice.

'No.' He shook his head with a soft smile. 'I gave myself time.'

'You gave *me* time,' she corrected.

His smile grew. 'Oh, sweetheart, you're no rescue package. I did it for both of us.'

Lorelei stood there for a timeless moment.

'Then why couldn't you love me?'

It was a plea from her heart.

'God, Lorelei.' It was wrenched from him. 'I was afraid I'd love you too much.'

Time stood still.

'I was a clingy kid,' he said, almost tonelessly. 'Dad had a stream of women in the early days, and whichever woman picked me up she'd be mum. But they'd always leave. Dad would drive them away with his drinking.'

Lorelei didn't shift an inch, afraid if she did he would stop. She so desperately wanted to hear it all, even as her mind turned in horror from the picture he was painting.

'The old man used to say they left because of me.' He shook his head at her expression. 'It's bull, I know. But when you're a kid you believe your dad.'

'Nash—' She reached up and stroked his face, unable not to touch him.

'When I went back to Sydney and saw the shape Jack was in his ex-wife said the same thing. *He's this way because of you.* And in a way she was right. I succeeded. I got the career, the money, the accolades. Jack couldn't cope.' He looked her in the eye. 'I looked at you, Lorelei, and all I saw was a fragile girl who'd run up debts and was living like there was no tomorrow.'

'C'est vrai,' she said softly. It was true. She had been.

'I knew you'd been through the wringer with that trial and all the nasty publicity, and I thought if I put you in the public eye it would be as if I'd turned a hunter's spotlight on you. All the stuff about your father would come out. For all those reasons I couldn't do it to you. I thought I'd break you. Just like I broke Jack.'

Lorelei shook her head.

'Then I saw you at the equestrian centre and I knew I'd got it wrong.'

She waited.

'All my life people have put my success down to natural gifts, and, yeah, I've got some talent. But I've worked damn hard to get where I am.

When you told me about your accident I knew we were alike. I understood you'd worked hard at your sport. I assumed you'd given it up. But when I saw you'd turned your dream into something better—something outward, for other people—I recognised what I already knew. You're a special woman, Lorelei St James. Then I did some phoning around. Why in the hell didn't you tell me those debts were your father's legal fees?'

Lorelei swallowed. 'I didn't tell anyone. I was ashamed.'

'You should be bloody proud. Your father is a lucky man. I kept telling myself you were like Jack—I'd overwhelm you, wreck your life—but the truth is you're strong. You're the strongest person I've ever met. Stronger than me. You overwhelm me.'

Stunned by this outpouring, Lorelei didn't know what to say. Nash, who never said more than he had to, hadn't stopped talking, and he was calling her special and strong and all the things she'd always wanted to be to someone but somehow never had been.

But all of this praise, all of this putting her on a pedestal, frightened her.

'Please don't turn me into a trophy. I'm flesh and blood—prone to mistakes, to overreacting...'

'No.' He shook his head vigorously, taking hold of her. 'No, I've never seen you as a trophy, Lorelei. I only said that because I didn't want it to be any different than what I'd known before. But it already was. From the moment we met. And that passion of yours—I never want you to lose it.'

'You broke our date!' She knew it was a small thing, but suddenly it assumed the huge dimensions it had always held inside her head and heart. Because she hadn't completely trusted him after that, and when he'd let her down she'd been half expecting it.

She needed to know why.

'Call it a last-ditch attempt to throw myself across the track. I knew even then I would love you to distraction. That night when I was coming out of that bar, and you were going in, I was on my way to see you.'

He loved her *to distraction?*

'You were?' Lorelei felt a rush of warmth dispelling the last of the coldness that had been dwelling within her these last two days. 'I wish you'd told me. I wish this had all been different....'

'It *is* different. God, Lorelei, I can't lose you. Nothing matters to me if you're not there to share it with me. It was never so clear to me as it was today. That race—I was numb. And then I saw you, and suddenly it was clear as light.'

Her heart thrummed and started beating to a slower, truer beat.

'You were right—what you said that night in Mauritius. The racing was never the point, I was empty, and I found you, and the emptiness went away. I knew I loved you. Deep down I knew it. Every which way I tried to figure it, I kept coming back to this selfish need I had to keep you with me. I kept telling myself you wouldn't cope, but it was *me*.'

He lowered his voice. 'I was so afraid of building a life around you and you walking away. I wasn't prepared to risk it.'

Lorelei laid her hand over his heart.

'All I want is to love you,' she said softly, sincerely. 'If you'll let me.'

He caught her up fiercely in his arms and for a long time just held on to her. Lorelei thought about the little boy who had craved love, the man he had grown into who had avoided it and its painful associations, and the man standing before her now, holding her so tightly, as if she were as vital to him as the blood in his veins, the air he breathed.

As he was to her.

He loved her for who she was, not who he wanted her to be.

It was a miracle.

Suddenly sobbing for breath, she framed his face tightly with her hands. 'Wherever you go, wherever you are, that's where I'll be. I won't leave you, I won't betray you and I won't stop loving you.'

Nash wrapped her in his arms and kissed her. She could feel him shaking slightly, feel the groundswell of feeling behind the sensual motion of his mouth against hers.

He rested his temple on hers.

'Just let me love you,' he said simply, his deep voice shaking with the force of his emotion.

'Ah, oui,' she whispered. 'I can do that, too.'

It was on a rare sunbathed morning in April when Lorelei stepped out into the gardens of the villa.

A great deal had changed in these parts in six months. A ridiculous amount of money had been poured into restoring the Spanish villa to its original grandeur, and its gardens once more lay in variegated parterres. The fountains sprang to life as the bride joined her father at the top of the steps. Lorelei held one section of her long ivory skirts aloft as she laid her other hand in the crook of her father's arm.

'Are you certain, *ma chère?* Nothing is set in stone.'

Lorelei smiled. 'But it is, *Papa*. It was the moment I set eyes on him.'

Raymond sighed. 'I suspected as much. So it is *l'amour* and I gain a very rich son-in-law.'

Lorelei's laughter sang them down the steps. She paused only to pluck a spray of her grandmother's lavender and tuck it into Raymond's lapel.

He had been released from prison shortly before Christmas, and was living quietly in Fiesole with wife number five—an older Italian widow with far too much money and a very good accountant. Lorelei was fairly sure Raymond was safe from his own light-fingered proclivities.

Nash waited restlessly with a small congregation of friends and family on the lawn of the old villa. Beyond was the view of Monaco made famous the world over in a much-loved film and the blue curve of the Mediterranean sea.

For the first time in months he hadn't slept in their bed here at home. He'd been relegated to a suite at the Hotel de Paris, which held special memories for them both.

This morning he'd dressed in a cutaway coat and striped tie, and had had his shoes polished whilst his brother Jack ribbed him about those who stood tallest falling hardest. At ten o'clock he'd climbed into the vintage Bugatti and took off up the hill.

This was the most important date of his life, and after every stumbling block he'd faced getting her here the sight of Lorelei coming towards him beneath a fine veil of valenciennes lace almost overwhelmed him.

Nash felt Jack's hand grip his arm briefly.

He nodded and blew out a deep breath.

He reached out his hand as Lorelei approached and she took it. Her fingers were trembling, but his were sure.

The officiant took them through the vows, pronounced them man and wife, and as he took Lorelei in his arms he knew exactly what all the fuss was about.

'Why, Nash, you're trembling,' she said with a little smile just for him.

'Just wait until I get you alone, Mrs Blue,' he replied.

'I can hardly wait,' she whispered.

Nash grinned. Yeah, that was one way of putting it.

And that was when the kissing started.

* * * * *

Mills & Boon® Large Print
June 2013

SOLD TO THE ENEMY
Sarah Morgan

UNCOVERING THE SILVERI SECRET
Melanie Milburne

BARTERING HER INNOCENCE
Trish Morey

DEALING HER FINAL CARD
Jennie Lucas

IN THE HEAT OF THE SPOTLIGHT
Kate Hewitt

NO MORE SWEET SURRENDER
Caitlin Crews

PRIDE AFTER HER FALL
Lucy Ellis

HER ROCKY MOUNTAIN PROTECTOR
Patricia Thayer

THE BILLIONAIRE'S BABY SOS
Susan Meier

BABY OUT OF THE BLUE
Rebecca Winters

BALLROOM TO BRIDE AND GROOM
Kate Hardy

0513 Rom LP

Mills & Boon® Large Print

July 2013

PLAYING THE DUTIFUL WIFE
Carol Marinelli

THE FALLEN GREEK BRIDE
Jane Porter

A SCANDAL, A SECRET, A BABY
Sharon Kendrick

THE NOTORIOUS GABRIEL DIAZ
Cathy Williams

A REPUTATION FOR REVENGE
Jennie Lucas

CAPTIVE IN THE SPOTLIGHT
Annie West

TAMING THE LAST ACOSTA
Susan Stephens

GUARDIAN TO THE HEIRESS
Margaret Way

LITTLE COWGIRL ON HIS DOORSTEP
Donna Alward

MISSION: SOLDIER TO DADDY
Soraya Lane

WINNING BACK HIS WIFE
Melissa McClone